A CAVALCADE OF QUEENS

A CAVALCADE OF

QUEENS

COLLECTED AND EDITED JOINTLY BY

ELEANOR FARJEON

AND

WILLIAM MAYNE

ILLUSTRATED BY

VICTOR AMBRUS

New York

HENRY Z. WALCK, INCORPORATED

1965

First published in Great Britain 1965
as *The Hamish Hamilton Book of Queens*

Library of Congress Catalog Card Number: 65-23251

Dedication

For Sarah, who, when feeling old
Got up and married and left the fold;
And Alexandra, in the position
Of studying hard to be a physician;
And for a younger sister, Deborah,
Who can ride a horse or gallop a zebborah;
And last and loudest, for Bryony Jane,
From Eleanor Farjeon and William Mayne.

PRINTED IN THE UNITED STATES OF AMERICA

Contents

Acknowledgements

We wish to thank the agents, publishers and executors who granted permission to reprint works by the following authors:

EDWARD THOMAS

Half a Loaf is Better than No Bread, reprinted from FOUR AND TWENTY BLACKBIRDS by permission of The Bodley Head Ltd.

WALTER DE LA MARE

Gone and *There Sate Good Queen Bess*, reprinted by permission of the Literary Trustees of Walter de la Mare and The Society of Authors as their representative.

ROBERT GRAVES

Henry and Mary, reprinted from THE PENNY FIDDLE, published by Cassell & Co. Ltd. and Doubleday & Co. Inc., New York, by permission of International Authors N.V.

RUDYARD KIPLING

Gloriana, reprinted from REWARDS AND FAIRIES, by permission of Mrs. George Bambridge and Macmillan & Co. Ltd., and the Macmillan Co. of Canada Ltd.

B. H. CHAMBERLAIN

The Silly Jelly-Fish. We have been unable to trace the owner of the copyright in this work, and we should therefore like to take this opportunity of apologizing to such person or persons for any inadvertent infringement of copyright which may occur through its publication in this book.

ELEANOR FARJEON

The Miracle of the Poor Island from THE LITTLE BOOKROOM, published by Oxford University Press, and by Henry Z. Walck, Inc., reprinted by permission of David Higham Associates Ltd.

Introduction

A Company of Queens

I

Queen
a queen
The Queen!

WORDS first enter our ears as sounds without sense. The senseless sounds are repeated over and over again by our mothers and nurses: *ma-ma, da-da, pussy, bow-wow, tweet!* To one and all of these our response is probably *goo-goo*. Our parents are enchanted by our cleverness.

Presently the Sounds, by constant repetition, turn into Images. They take shape as the soft presence that cuddles us in her arms, the strong one that tosses us in the air, the tiny one that hops inside a cage; we echo the Sounds and say *Ma-ma* to the cuddler, *Da-da* to the tosser, *Tweet!* to the tiny thing that, let out of the cage, has settled on *ma-ma's* finger. Our parents are amazed by our intelligence.

At last, in our budding minds, the Images flower into Ideas. It isn't the sounds or even the images, it is the ideas they evoke which are the heart and soul of a child's interior world; the world to which our parents have no clue, the world we continue to dwell in when the lights are out, and our eyes no longer see the shapes we already know as dog, bird, cat, as father and mother. In every child the idea of a dog, a bird, a cat, and especially father and mother, is different, as it takes colour from our own experience. Yet each of these ideas began for all of us in the same way: as sound without sense or meaning. From this moment onward the ideas that people our secret world begin to enlarge themselves; born of a seed of sound, they grow with us as we grow, and change as we change.

But Queen! What can be done about Queen? She never began as a mere sound. How does a queen, how does even THE Queen, manage to take her place inside that world? My first idea of Queen came to me from—where? A picture-book? A nursery-rhyme?

The Queen was in the parlour
Eating bread-and-honey . . .

Perhaps I myself now knew the taste of honey—ah! so the Queen was someone who, like me, stickied her mouth with honey at the tea-table. Only the Queen didn't sit up to table on a high chair; for when my pussy-cat went to London to visit her, she sat on something bigger called a throne. The idea of Queen was already enlarging itself. I must have been three or four years old before it separated into two quite different images. One was Queen Victoria on the throne of England. The other the Fairy Queen on top of the Christmas Tree.

II

My two Queens did not meet, each kept to her own kingdom, and never crossed the other one's boundaries. But the real and ideal kingdoms which they ruled in my world in the dark extended their boundaries year by year, as Victoria's realm spread backward into History, and the Fairy Queen's flowed onward into Poetry. It was Poetry's way to enlarge by revelation, while History increased itself by association. Poetry said, "Have faith!"—and I had faith in the magic of fairies. History said, "Believe!"—and I believed in Queen Victoria. She was History's guarantee that queens were as real as I was. She sat like a signpost on History's road at the point it had reached in 1881, the year when I was born. I could not imagine any other queen ruling the land I actually lived in. Her powerful little presence possessed the English throne with a sort of immortality that made it hard to believe queens ever died. And yet, they did. Her plump finger pointed behind her to queens who had once been as real as she was now: to Queen Anne, Queen Elizabeth, Queen Mary, queens who had sat in their own right on her very throne, and held her very sceptre, and worn her very crown: and then to the lesser queens of kings who had worn the crown. Some of these had even borne my name.

They were the first historical queens who really *mattered* to me. I was Eleanor, Eleanor was Me. My name became crowded with identities. Eleanor of Aquitaine (how I disliked her!) Eleanor of Castile (whom I adored). She and I were one. King Edward the First, the tallest King in English History, was my husband. It was I who sucked the poison from his wound on the battlefield—yes, I might have died! It was for me, when I did die, that he raised the Crosses from end to end of England, wherever my fair body rested as it passed on its way to the tomb. They were called Eleanor Crosses. I, of course, was looking on—or was it down?—from some point of vantage in heaven, and heard the sobs of the populace, and saw Edward dash the tears from his manly eyes as he halted the procession to erect yet another Cross. When I and my brothers went for summer holidays in Kent, the jostling children in the station didn't know that Charing Cross was an Eleanor Cross, *my* Cross!

But Eleanor of Aquitaine remained a thorn in my flesh. Not only didn't she suck the poison from her husband's wound, she was herself a poisoner! She tried to poison Fair Rosamond in her Bower, beloved of the King. So said Lord Tennyson, and who should know if not the Poet-Laureate? But much as I hated the Aquitaine Eleanor, my name—bother it!—took colour from hers. No getting away from it, she was once a queen as real as Queen Victoria.

Never mind, Victoria IS the Queen, God save her! Her picture is on my Jubilee Geography Atlas, her face is on every penny with which I buy four pink sugar mice, she has a purple face on the postage-stamp we stick on letters, a red face on the ha'penny stamp we stick on postcards. On her Jubilee in 1887, when I was six years old, we made gold-paper crowns and sceptres in our nursery, and walked with them round the rosebeds in the garden, and set up a throne under the cherry-tree. We let little Marie Barnes sit on the throne, and we bowed to her. This generosity was because little Marie wasn't quite like us, or any of our other small friends. There was something that stopped her from understanding things as we understood them, so we made her Queen Victoria on Jubilee Day. As we could not see the Procession that was passing through the decorated streets of London, we had our own Procession in the garden, and crowned little Marie with gold paper, and kissed her hand. She grew pink, and tittered with pleasure. She was the Queen!

Ten years afterwards, on Diamond Jubilee Day, we all went to a grand house near Hyde Park Corner, and looked down from big windows at the glittering procession of Kings and Princes and Generals passing through the humming streets below. After the soldiers and sailors of England, and the Kings of Europe in their uniforms, came an open carriage, with the little old Queen in black and her widow's bonnet. She was murmuring, "So kind! so kind!" as she drove through the cheering crowds; but of course we couldn't hear her, we were too far away. We had specially nice things to eat and drink, cold salmon and strawberries and iced lemonade, before we went home.

Three more years went by. One night we were in the light green Atlas omnibus on the way to a theatre. "Suddenly" (I wrote later) "the air was rent with the newsboys' cries. Papa said to Mama, 'We must go home, there'll be no performance tonight.' Queen Victoria was dead. I remember how this shook my universe . . . inside the bus I sat clasping my hands, saying some sort of vague prayer for the Queen, and thinking, 'Something big has happened' " . . . So even Queens could die, even the Queen who had been for ever in my twenty years of life. Things would be different with a King on the throne. And very soon they were. Queen Victoria was with the Queens of History, with Anne and Elizabeth and Mary and Eleanor of Castile. However long they may reign, the Queens of History are mortal, just like us.

III

And the Fairy Queen on the Christmas-tree, what about her? She was immortal, that was the difference I had known since I was four years old. I did not know that she owed her kingdom in my world in the dark to a mortal queen I had not heard of then. Queen Charlotte, the wife of King George the Third, had come from the land of fir-trees and fairy-tales. In Germany Christmas without a tree was not to be thought of, *na, das war undenkbar!* So the first Christmas-tree ever dressed in England was set up in Buckingham Palace; and after that the great and humble homes of England followed suit.

In our own middle-class home in Adelaide Road, the day the Christmas-tree came from the Army and Navy Stores was second only in excitement to Christmas Day itself. Papa always went to choose the biggest the Stores could provide; some ten or twelve feet had to be cut off before the great fir-tree could be stood upright in the drawing-room, which it half filled with the spread of its lower branches. To my brothers and myself, hidden from each other as we ran around it, sniffing the dark recesses rapturously, it was as though a forest had invaded the house. After that first sight it was kept locked away from us for two weeks; when we saw it next on Christmas morning, the forest had become a world of glittering toys and sparkling trinkets, the kingdom of the Fairy Queen on top whose wings touched the ceiling: the Queen with blue glass eyes, rosy waxen cheeks, silky gold hair, gauze skirts and silver wand, for whom all the little girls' hearts swelled with longing under their party frocks. Our Christmas parties were renowned among our friends who went home laden with toys and sweets and picture-books; no little girl went away without a doll but only one could have the Fairy Queen. She was not reserved for the daughter of the house; when the party was over, my father would mount a ladder hidden behind the tree, and fetch the fairy down for one of my lucky friends. I remember once being the lucky child at another party, and bringing home a Fairy Queen to reign in our nursery. Yet for all her magic I can't remember her outlasting the commoners in the toy-cupboard, the stuffed rag dolls, the china dolls with glossy faces and sawdust bodies, the wooden dolls with painted hair and cheeks. All too soon the queens of toyland went the way of all wax, and one day vanished—to die?

Of course not! The Toyland Queens lived on in the Land of Pantomime; Fairy Queens, not of wax, but of flesh and blood. They sang, they danced, they waved their star-lit wands, quelling demons with glittering eyelids who cowered at their feet, and before the curtain fell, bringing about the triumph of Good over Evil, in a Transformation Scene of transcendent beauty. When heroines were saved and villains foiled, there reigned the Queen at the heart of this sparkling scene, the Fairy without whom Cinderella would for ever go in rags, the Sleeping Beauty be for ever unawakened, and Snow-White for ever silent in her glass coffin. For a few more years of my childhood, the Pantomime Queens upheld immortal Fairydom.

Alas, as I grew older, even the pantomime glories began to dim, and the annual excitement lessened. We didn't believe in Fairy Queens any more, and Peter Pan had not then been born to demand, year after year, that we should. And if he had been, what would have been the use? We should not have *believed*; only agreed to believe, which is not the same thing.

What was left for faith? Was magic only a box of tricks after all? Was nothing immortal under the visiting moon? Where was my Fairy Queen who would not die, when pantomime fairyland melted into thin air, and left not a rack behind?

Philomel with melody . . .

Poetry was left. A poet once turned his back on the world where mortal kings and queens are born, die, and have their dates put down in the history books. One midsummer night he filled his pen with moonshine and made it into an unfading fairyland. Oberon and Titania, its king and queen, are as real as the human beings they mingle with; they quarrel and love, make mischief and shed blessings, just like the kings and queens whose deaths are recorded in the history books. But Queen Titania's death goes unrecorded; she was born immortal of our poet's brain. And so she remains for me in my world in the dark, as radiant as when she first appeared there on a midsummer bank

"... where the wild thyme blows,
Where oxlips and the nodding violet grows;
Quite over-canopied with luscious woodbine,
With sweet musk-roses, and with eglantine;
There sleeps Titania sometime of the night,
Lull'd in these flowers with dances and delight;
And there the snake throws her enamell'd skin,
Weed wide enough to wrap a fairy in . . .

Philomel, with melody
Sing in our sweet lullaby;
Lulla, lulla, lullaby, lulla, lulla, lullaby:
Never harm
Nor spell, nor charm,
Come our lovely lady nigh;
So, good night, with lullaby."

ELEANOR FARJEON

The White Cat
and
Jackal or Tiger?

ANDREW LANG

Andrew Lang collected a great many fairy tales, in the books called the Blue Fairy Tale Book, *and the* Red, Green, *and other coloured ones. Here are two of them:* The White Cat *is from the* Blue *book and* Jackal or Tiger? *is from the* Olive *book. Lang wrote a great deal of other work, too, which you may come to in time. He loved to unravel historical puzzles, particularly about the Stuart Kings and Queens—and the other Stuarts who didn't quite succeed in becoming King or Queen (it's quite another story that they should have been). Apart from knowing what he wrote and what he was interested in, I know very little about him, whether he was tall or short, dark or fair, blue- or brown-eyed, whether he had a dog or a walking-stick or a black horse or a telescope. I should guess that he was tall, because Lang is Scottish for Long; and that he liked porridge, because he was Scottish himself. He knew a great many things, and wrote about them readably.*

His wife was Leonora Alleyne and she was also a writer. She translated many of the stories in Lang's books from the languages they were first written in.

W.M.

ONCE upon a time there was a King who had three sons, who were all so clever and brave that he began to be afraid that they would want to reign over the kingdom before he was dead. Now the King, though he felt that he was growing old, did not at all wish to give up the government of his kingdom while he could still manage it very well, so he thought the best way to live in peace would be to divert the minds of his sons by promises which he could always get out of when the time came for keeping them.

So he sent for them all, and, after speaking to them kindly, he added:

"You will quite agree with me, my dear children, that my great age makes it impossible for me to look after my affairs of state as carefully as I once did. I begin to fear that this may affect the welfare of my subjects, therefore I wish that one of you should succeed to my crown; but in return for such a gift as this it is only right that you should do something for me. Now, as I think of retiring into the country, it seems to me that a pretty, lively, faithful little dog would be very good company for me; so, without any regard for your ages, I promise that the one who brings me the most beautiful little dog shall succeed me at once."

The three Princes were greatly surprised by their father's sudden fancy for a little dog, but as it gave the two younger ones a chance they would not otherwise have had of being king, and as the eldest was too polite to make any objection, they accepted the commission with pleasure. They bade farewell to the King, who gave them presents of silver and precious stones, and appointed to meet them at the same hour, in the same place, after a year had passed, to see the little dogs they had brought for him.

Then they went together to a castle which was about a league from the city, accompanied by all their particular friends, to whom they gave a grand banquet, and the three brothers promised to be friends always, to share whatever good fortune befell them, and not to be parted by any envy or jealousy; and so they set out, agreeing to meet at the same castle at the appointed time, to present themselves before the King together. Each one took a different road, and the two eldest met with many adventures; but it is about the youngest that you are going to hear. He was young, and gay, and handsome, and knew everything that a prince ought to know; and as for his courage, there was simply no end of it.

Hardly a day passed without his buying several dogs—big and little, greyhounds, mastiffs, spaniels, and lapdogs. As soon as he had bought a pretty one he was sure to see a still prettier, and then he had to get rid of all the others and buy that one, as, being alone, he found it impossible to take thirty or forty thousand dogs about with him. He journeyed from day to day, not knowing where he was going, until at last, just at nightfall, he reached a great, gloomy forest. He did not know his way, and, to make matters worse, it began to thunder, and the rain poured down. He took the first path he could find, and after walking for a long time he fancied he saw a faint light, and began to hope that he was coming to some cottage where he might find shelter for the night. At length, guided by the light, he reached the door of the most splendid castle he could have imagined. This door was of gold covered with carbuncles, and it was the pure red light which shone from them that had shown him the way through the forest. The walls were of the finest porcelain in all the most delicate colours, and the Prince saw that all the stories he had ever read were pictured upon them; but as he was quite terribly wet, and the rain still fell in torrents, he could not stay to look about any more, but came back to the golden door. There he saw a deer's foot hanging by a chain of diamonds, and he began to wonder who could live in this magnificent castle.

"They must feel very secure against robbers," he said to himself. "What is to hinder anyone from cutting off that chain and digging out those carbuncles, and making himself rich for life?"

He pulled the deer's foot, and immediately a silver bell sounded and the door flew open, but the Prince could see nothing but numbers of hands in the air, each holding a torch. He was so much surprised that he stood quite still, until he felt himself pushed forward by other hands, so that, though he was somewhat uneasy, he could not help going on. With his hand on his sword, to be prepared for whatever might happen, he entered a hall paved with lapis-lazuli, while two lovely voices sang:

"The hands you see floating above
Will swiftly your bidding obey;
If your heart dreads not conquering Love,
In this place you may fearlessly stay."

The Prince could not believe that any danger threatened him when he was welcomed in this way, so, guided by the mysterious hands, he went towards a door of coral, which opened of its own accord, and he found himself in a vast hall of mother-of-pearl, out of which opened a number of other rooms, glittering with thousands of lights, and full of such beautiful pictures and precious things that the

Prince felt quite bewildered. After passing through sixty rooms the hands that conducted him stopped, and the Prince saw a most comfortable-looking arm-chair drawn up close to the chimney-corner; at the same moment the fire lighted itself, and the pretty, soft, clever hands took off the Prince's wet, muddy clothes, and presented him with fresh ones made of the richest stuffs, all embroidered with gold and emeralds. He could not help admiring everything he saw, and the deft way in which the hands waited on him, though they sometimes appeared so suddenly that they made him jump.

When he was quite ready—and I can assure you that he looked very different from the wet and weary Prince who had stood outside in the rain, and pulled the deer's foot—the hands led him to a splendid room, upon the walls of which were painted the histories of Puss in Boots and a number of other famous cats. The table was laid for supper with two golden plates, and golden spoons and forks, and the sideboard was covered with dishes and glasses of crystal set with precious stones. The Prince was wondering who the second place could be for, when suddenly in came about a dozen cats carrying guitars and rolls of music, who took their places at one end of the room, and under the direction of a cat who beat time with a roll of paper began to mew in every imaginable key, and to draw their claws across the strings of the guitars, making the strangest kind of music that could be heard. The Prince hastily stopped up his ears, but even then the sight of these comical musicians sent him into fits of laughter.

"What funny thing shall I see next?" he said to himself, and instantly the door opened, and in came a tiny figure covered by a long black veil. It was conducted by two cats wearing black mantles and carrying swords, and a

large party of cats followed, who brought in cages full of rats and mice.

The Prince was so much astonished that he thought he must be dreaming, but the little figure came up to him and threw back its veil, and he saw that it was the loveliest little white cat it is possible to imagine. She looked very young and very sad, and in a sweet little voice that went straight to his heart she said to the Prince:

"King's son, you are welcome; the Queen of the Cats is glad to see you."

"Lady Cat," replied the Prince, "I thank you for receiving me so kindly, but surely you are no ordinary pussy-cat? Indeed, the way you speak and the magnificence of your castle prove it plainly."

"King's son," said the White Cat, "I beg you to spare me these compliments, for I am not used to them. But now," she added, "let supper be served, and let the musicians be silent, as the Prince does not understand what they are saying."

So the mysterious hands began to bring in the supper, and first they put on the table two dishes, one containing stewed pigeons and the other a fricassee of fat mice. The sight of the latter made the Prince feel as if he could not enjoy his supper at all; but the White Cat seeing this assured him that the dishes intended for him were prepared in a separate kitchen, and he might be quite certain that they contained neither rats nor mice; and the Prince felt so sure that she would not deceive him that he had no more hesitation in beginning. Presently he noticed that on the little paw that was next him the White Cat wore a bracelet containing a portrait, and he begged to be allowed to look at it. To his great surprise he found it represented an extremely handsome young man, who was so like himself that it might have been his own portrait! The White

Cat sighed as he looked at it, and seemed sadder than ever, and the Prince dared not ask any questions for fear of displeasing her; so he began to talk about other things, and found that she was interested in all the subjects he cared for himself, and seemed to know quite well what was going on in the world. After supper they went into another room, which was fitted up as a theatre, and the cats acted and danced for their amusement, and then the White Cat said good-night to him, and the hands conducted him into a room he had not seen before, hung with tapestry worked with butterflies' wings of every colour; there were mirrors that reached from the ceiling to the floor, and a little white bed with curtains of gauze tied up with ribbons. The Prince went to bed in silence, as he did not quite know how to begin a conversation with the hands that waited on him, and in the morning he was awakened by a noise and confusion outside his window, and the hands came and quickly dressed him in hunting costume. When he looked out all the cats were assembled in the courtyard, some leading greyhounds, some blowing horns, for the White Cat was going out hunting. The hands led a wooden horse up to the Prince, and seemed to expect him to mount it, at which he was very indignant; but it was no use for him to object, for he speedily found himself upon its back, and it pranced gaily off with him.

The White Cat herself was riding a monkey, which climbed even up to the eagles' nests when she had a fancy for the young eaglets. Never was there a pleasanter hunting party, and when they returned to the castle the Prince and the White Cat supped together as before, but when they had finished she offered him a crystal goblet, which must have contained a magic draught, for, as soon as he had swallowed its contents, he forgot everything, even the little dog that he was seeking for the King and only thought how happy he was to be with the White Cat! And so the days passed, in every kind of amusement, until the year was nearly gone. The Prince had forgotten all about meeting his brothers: he did not even know what country he belonged to; but the White Cat knew when he ought to go back, and one day she said to him:

"Do you know that you have only three days left to look for the little dog for your father, and your brothers have found lovely ones?"

Then the Prince suddenly recovered his memory, and cried:

"What can have made me forget such an important thing? My whole fortune depends upon it; and even if I could in such a short time find a dog pretty enough to gain me a kingdom, where should I find a horse who could carry me all that way in three days?" And he began to be very vexed. But the White Cat said to him: "King's son, do not trouble yourself; I am your friend, and will make everything easy for you. You can still stay here for a day, as the good wooden horse can take you to your country in twelve hours."

"I thank you, beautiful Cat," said the Prince; "but what good will it do me to get back if I have not a dog to take to my father?"

"See here," answered the White Cat, holding up an acorn; "there is a prettier one in this than in the Dog-star!"

"Oh! White Cat dear," said the Prince, "how unkind you are to laugh at me now!"

"Only listen," she said, holding the acorn to his ear.

And inside it he distinctly heard a tiny voice say: "Bow-wow!"

The Prince was delighted, for a dog that can be shut up in an acorn must be very small indeed. He wanted to take it out and look at it, but the White Cat said it would be better not to open the acorn till he was before the King, in case the tiny dog should be cold on the journey. He thanked her a thousand times, and said good-bye quite sadly when the time came for him to set out.

"The days have passed so quickly with you," he said, "I only wish I could take you with me now."

But the White Cat shook her head and sighed deeply in answer.

After all the Prince was the first to arrive at the castle where he had agreed to meet his brothers, but they came soon after, and stared in amazement when they saw the wooden horse in the courtyard jumping like a hunter.

The Prince met them joyfully, and they began to tell him all their adventures; but he managed to hide from them what he had been doing, and even led them to think that a turnspit dog which he had with him was the one he was bringing for the King. Fond as they all were of one another, the two eldest could not help being glad to think that their dogs certainly had a better chance. The next morning they started in the same chariot. The elder brothers carried in baskets two such tiny, fragile dogs that they hardly dared to touch them. As for the turnspit, he ran after the chariot, and got so covered with mud that one could hardly see what he was like at all. When they reached the palace everyone crowded round to welcome them as they went into the King's great hall; and when the two brothers presented their little dogs nobody could decide which was the prettier. They were already arranging between themselves to share the kingdom equally, when the youngest stepped forward, drawing from his

pocket the acorn the White Cat had given him. He opened it quickly, and there upon a white cushion they saw a dog so small that it could easily have been put through a ring. The Prince laid it upon the ground, and it got up at once and began to dance. The King did not know what to say, for it was impossible that anything could be prettier than this little creature. Nevertheless, as he was in no hurry to part with his crown, he told his sons that as they had been so successful the first time, he would ask them to go once again, and seek by land and sea for a piece of muslin so fine that it could be drawn through the eye of a needle. The brothers were not very willing to set out again, but the two eldest consented because it gave them another chance, and they started as before. The youngest again mounted the wooden horse, and rode back at full speed to his beloved White Cat. Every door of the castle stood wide open, and every window and turret was illuminated, so it looked more wonderful than before. The hands hastened to meet him, and led the wooden horse off to the stable, while he hurried in to find the White Cat. She was asleep in a little basket on a white satin cushion, but she very soon started up when she heard the Prince, and was overjoyed at seeing him once more.

"How could I hope that you would come back to me, King's son?" she said. And then he stroked and petted her, and told her of his successful journey, and how he had come back to ask her help, as he believed that it was impossible to find what the King demanded. The White Cat looked serious, and said she must think what was to be done, but that, luckily, there were some cats in the castle who could spin very well, and if anybody could manage it they could, and she would set them the task herself.

And then the hands appeared carrying torches and conducted the Prince and the White Cat to a long gallery which overlooked the river, from the windows of which they saw a magnificent display of fireworks of all sorts; after which they had supper, which the Prince liked even better than the fireworks, for it was very late, and he was hungry after his long ride. And so the days passed quickly as before; it was impossible to feel dull with the White Cat, and she had quite a talent for inventing new amusements—indeed, she was cleverer than a cat has a right to be. But when the Prince asked her how it was that she was so wise, she only said:

"King's son, do not ask me; guess what you please. I may not tell you anything."

The Prince was so happy that he did not trouble himself at all about the time, but presently the White Cat told him that the year was gone, and that he need not be at all anxious about the piece of muslin, as they had made it very well.

"This time," she added, "I can give you a suitable escort;" and on looking out into the courtyard the Prince saw a superb chariot of burnished gold, enamelled in flame colour with a thousand different devices. It was drawn by twelve snow-white horses, harnessed four abreast; their trappings were of flame-coloured velvet, embroidered with diamonds. A hundred chariots followed, each drawn by eight horses, and filled with officers in splendid uniforms, and a thousand guards surrounded the procession. "Go!" said the White Cat, "and when you appear before the King in such state he surely will not refuse you the crown which you deserve. Take this walnut, but do not open it until you are before him, then you will find in it the piece of stuff you asked me for."

"Lovely Blanchette," said the Prince, "how can I thank you properly for all your kindness to me? Only tell me that you wish it, and I will give up for ever all thought of being king, and will stay here with you always."

"King's son," she replied, "it shows the goodness of your heart that you should care so much for a little white cat, who is good for nothing but to catch mice; but you must not stay."

So the Prince kissed her little paw and set out. You can imagine how fast he travelled when I tell you that they reached the King's palace in just half the time it had taken the wooden horse to get there. This time the Prince was so late that he did not try to meet his brothers at their castle, so they thought he could not be coming, and were rather glad of it, and displayed their pieces of muslin to the King proudly, feeling sure of success. And indeed the stuff was very fine, and would go through the eye of a very large needle; but the King, who was only too glad to make a difficulty, sent for a particular needle, which was kept among the Crown jewels, and had such a small eye that everybody saw at once that it was impossible that the muslin should pass through it. The Princes were angry, and were beginning to complain that it was a trick, when suddenly the trumpets sounded and the youngest Prince came in. His father and brothers were quite astonished at his magnificence, and after he had greeted them he took the walnut from his pocket and opened it, fully expecting to find the piece of muslin, but instead there was only a hazel-nut. He cracked it, and there lay a cherry-stone. Everybody was looking on, and the King was chuckling to himself at the idea of finding the piece of muslin in a nut-shell.

However, the Prince cracked the cherry-stone, but everyone laughed when he saw it contained only its own kernel. He opened that and found a grain of wheat, and in that was a millet seed. Then he himself began to wonder, and muttered softly:

"White Cat, White Cat, are you making fun of me?"

In an instant he felt a cat's claw give his hand quite a sharp scratch, and hoping that it was meant as an encouragement he opened the millet seed, and drew out of it a piece of muslin four hundred ells long, woven with the loveliest colours and most wonderful patterns; and when the needle was brought it went through the eye six times with the greatest ease! The King turned pale, and the other Princes stood silent and sorrowful, for nobody could deny that this was the most marvellous piece of muslin that was to be found in the world.

Presently the King turned to his sons, and said, with a deep sigh:

"Nothing could console me more in my old age than to realise your willingness to gratify my wishes. Go then once more, and whoever at the end of a year can bring back the loveliest princess shall be married to her, and shall, without further delay, receive the crown, for my successor must certainly be married." The Prince considered that he had earned the kingdom fairly twice over, but still he was too well bred to argue about it, so he just went back to his gorgeous chariot, and, surrounded by his escort, returned to the White Cat faster than he had come. This time she was expecting him, the path was strewn with flowers, and a thousand braziers were burning scented woods which perfumed the air. Seated in a gallery from which she could see his arrival, the White Cat waited for him. "Well, King's son," she said, "here you are once more, without a crown." "Madam," said he, "thanks to your generosity I have earned one twice over; but the fact is that my father is so loath to part with it that it would be no pleasure to me to take it."

"Never mind," she answered; "it's just as well to try and deserve it. As you must take back a lovely princess with you next time I will be on the look-out for one for you. In the meantime let us enjoy ourselves; tonight I have ordered a battle between my cats and the river rats, on purpose to amuse you." So this year slipped away even more pleasantly than the preceding ones. Sometimes the Prince could not help asking the White Cat how it was she could talk.

"Perhaps you are a fairy," he said. "Or has some enchanter changed you into a cat?"

But she only gave him answers that told him nothing. Days go by so quickly when one is very happy that it is certain the Prince would never have thought of its being time to go back, when one evening as they sat together the White Cat said to him that if he wanted to take a lovely princess home with him the next day he must be prepared to do as she told him.

"Take this sword," she said, "and cut off my head!"

"I!" cried the Prince, "I cut off your head! Blanchette darling, how could I do it?"

"I entreat you to do as I tell you, King's son," she replied.

The tears came into the Prince's eyes as he begged her to ask him anything but that—to set him any task she pleased as a proof of his devotion, but to spare him the grief of killing his dear Pussy. But nothing he could say altered her determination, and at last he drew his sword, and desperately, with a trembling hand, cut off the little white head. But imagine his astonishment and delight when suddenly a lovely princess stood before him, and, while he was still speechless with amazement, the door opened and a goodly company of knights and ladies entered, each carrying a cat's skin! They hastened with every sign of joy to the Princess, kissing her hand and congratulating her on being once more restored to her natural shape. She received them graciously, but after a few minutes begged that they would leave her alone with the Prince, to whom she said:

"You see, Prince, that you were right in supposing me to be no ordinary cat. My father reigned over six kingdoms. The Queen, my mother, whom he loved dearly, had a passion for travelling and exploring, and when I was only a few weeks old she obtained his permission to visit a certain mountain of which she had heard many marvellous tales, and set out, taking with her a number of her attendants. On the way they had to pass near an old castle belonging to the fairies. Nobody had ever been into it, but it was reported to be full of the most wonderful things, and my mother remembered to have heard that the fairies had in their garden such fruits as were to be seen and tasted nowhere else. She began to wish to try them for herself, and turned her steps in the direction of the garden. On arriving at the door, which blazed with gold and jewels she ordered her servants to knock loudly, but it was useless; it seemed as if all the inhabitants of the castle must be asleep or dead. Now the more difficult it became to obtain the fruit, the more the Queen was determined that have it she would. So she ordered that they should bring ladders, and get over the wall into the garden; but though the wall did not look very high and they tied the ladders together to make them very long, it was quite impossible to get to the top.

"The Queen was in despair, but as night was coming on she ordered that they should encamp just where they were, and went to bed herself, feeling quite ill, she was so disappointed. In the middle of the night she was suddenly awakened, and saw to her surprise a tiny, ugly old woman seated by her bedside, who said to her:

" 'I must say that we consider it somewhat troublesome of your Majesty to insist upon tasting our fruit; but, to save you any annoyance, my sisters and I will consent to give you as much as you can carry away, on one condition —that is, that you shall give us your little daughter to bring up as our own.'

" 'Ah! my dear madam,' cried the Queen, 'is there nothing else that you will take for the fruit? I will give you my kingdoms willingly.'

" 'No,' replied the old fairy, 'we will have nothing but your little daughter. She shall be as happy as the day is long, and we will give her everything that is worth having in fairyland, but you must not see her again until she is married.'

" 'Though it is a hard condition,' said the Queen, 'I consent, for I shall certainly die if I do not taste the fruit, and so I should lose my little daughter either way.'

"So the old fairy led her into the castle, and, though it was still the middle of the night, the Queen could see plainly that it was far more beautiful than she had been told, which you can easily believe, Prince," said the White Cat, "when I tell you that it was this castle that we are now in. 'Will you gather the fruit yourself, Queen?' said the old fairy, 'or shall I call it to come to you?'

" 'I beg you to let me see it come when it is called,' cried the Queen; 'that will be something quite new.' The old fairy whistled twice, then she cried:

" 'Apricots, peaches, nectarines, cherries, plums, pears, melons, grapes, apples, oranges, lemons, gooseberries, strawberries, raspberries come!'

"And in an instant they came tumbling in, one over another, and yet they were neither dusty nor spoilt, and the Queen found them quite as good as she had fancied them. You see they grew upon fairy trees.

"The old fairy gave her golden caskets in which to take the fruit away, and it was as much as four hundred mules could carry. Then she reminded the Queen of her agreement, and led her back to the camp, and next morning she went back to her kingdom; but before she had gone very far she began to repent of her bargain, and when the King came out to meet her she looked so sad that he guessed that something had happened, and asked what was the matter. At first the Queen was afraid to tell him, but when, as soon as they reached the palace, five frightful little dwarfs were sent by the fairies to fetch me, she was obliged to confess what she had promised. The King was very angry, and had the Queen and myself shut up in a great tower and safely guarded, and drove the little dwarfs out of his kingdom; but the fairies sent a great dragon who ate up all the people he met, and whose breath burnt up everything as he passed through the country; and at last, after trying in vain to rid himself of the monster, the King, to save his subjects, was obliged to consent that I should be given up to the fairies. This time they came themselves to fetch me, in a chariot of pearl drawn by sea-horses, followed by the dragon, who was led with chains of diamonds. My cradle was placed between the old fairies, who loaded me with caresses, and away we whirled through the air to a tower which they had built on purpose for me. There I grew up surrounded with everything that was beautiful and rare, and learning everything that is ever taught to a princess, but without any companions, except a parrot and a little dog who could both talk; and receiving every day a visit from one of the old fairies, who came mounted upon the dragon. One day, however, as I sat at my window I saw a handsome young prince, who seemed to have been hunting in the forest which surrounded my prison, and who was standing and looking up at me. When he saw that I observed him he saluted me with great deference. You can imagine that I was delighted to have some one new to talk to, and in spite of the height of my window our conversation was prolonged till night fell, then my prince reluctantly bade me farewell. But after that he came again many times, and at last I consented to marry him, but the question was how I was to escape from my tower. The fairies always supplied me with flax for my spinning, and by great diligence I made enough cord for a ladder that would reach to the foot of the tower; but, alas! just as my prince was helping me to descend it, the crossest and ugliest of the old fairies flew in. Before he had time to defend himself my unhappy lover was swallowed up by the dragon. As for me, the fairies, furious at having their plans defeated, for they intended me to marry the king of the dwarfs and I utterly refused, changed me into a white cat. When they brought me here I found all the lords and ladies of my father's court awaiting me under the same enchantment, while the people of lesser rank had been made invisible, all but their hands.

"As they laid me under the enchantment the fairies told me all my history, for until then I had quite believed that I was their child, and warned me that my only chance of regaining my natural form was to win the love of a prince who resembled in every way my unfortunate lover."

"And you have won it, lovely Princess," interrupted the Prince.

"You are indeed wonderfully like him," resumed the Princess—"in voice, in features, and everything; and if you really love me all my troubles will be at an end."

"And mine too," cried the Prince, throwing himself at her feet, "if you will consent to marry me."

"I love you already better than anyone in the world," she said; "but now it is time go back to your father, and we shall hear what he says about it."

So the Prince gave her his hand and led her out, and they mounted the chariot together; it was even more splendid than before, and so was the whole company. Even the horses' shoes were of rubies with diamond nails, and I suppose that is the first time such a thing was ever seen.

As the Princess was as kind and clever as she was beautiful, you may imagine what a delightful journey the Prince found it, for everything the Princess said seemed to him quite charming.

When they came near the castle where the brothers were to meet, the Princess got into a chair carried by four of the guards; it was hewn out of one splendid crystal, and had silken curtains, which she drew round her that she might not be seen.

The Prince saw his brothers walking upon the terrace, each with a lovely princess, and they came to meet him, asking if he had also found a wife. He said that he had found something much rarer—a little white cat! At which they laughed very much, and asked him if he was afraid of being eaten up by mice in the palace. And then they set out together for the town. Each prince and princess rode in a splendid carriage; the horses were decked with plumes of feathers, and glittered with gold. After them came the youngest prince, and last of all the crystal chair, at which everybody looked with admiration and curiosity. When the courtiers saw them coming they hastened to tell the King.

"Are the ladies beautiful?" he asked anxiously.

And when they answered that nobody had ever before seen such lovely princesses he seemed quite annoyed.

However, he received them graciously, but found it impossible to choose between them.

Then turning to his youngest son he said:

"Have you come back alone, after all?"

"Your Majesty," replied the Prince, "will find in that crystal chair a little white cat, which has such soft paws, and mews so prettily, that I am sure you will be charmed with it."

The King smiled, and went to draw back the curtains himself, but at a touch from the Princess the crystal shivered into a thousand splinters, and there she stood in all her beauty; her fair hair floated over her shoulders and was crowned with flowers, and her softly falling robe was of the purest white. She saluted the King gracefully, while a murmur of admiration rose from all around.

"Sire," she said, "I am not come to deprive you of the throne you fill so worthily. I have already six kingdoms, permit me to bestow one upon you, and upon each of your sons. I ask nothing but your friendship, and your consent to my marriage with your youngest son; we shall still have three kingdoms left for ourselves."

The King and all the courtiers could not conceal their joy and astonishment, and the marriage of the three Princes was celebrated at once. The festivities lasted several months, and then each king and queen departed to their own kingdom and lived happily ever after.

Jackal or Tiger?

ONE hot night, in Hindustan, a King and Queen lay awake in the palace in the midst of the city. Every now and then a faint air blew through the lattice, and they hoped they were going to sleep, but they never did. Presently they became more broad awake than ever at the sound of a howl outside the palace.

"Listen to that tiger!" remarked the King.

"Tiger?" replied the Queen. "How should there be a tiger inside the city? It was only a jackal."

"I tell you it was a tiger," said the King.

"And I tell you that you were dreaming if you thought it was anything but a jackal," answered the Queen.

"I say it was a tiger," cried the King: "don't contradict me."

"Nonsense!" snapped the Queen. "It was a jackal." And the dispute waxed so warm that the King said at last;

"Very well, we'll call the guard and ask; and if it was a jackal I'll leave this kingdom to you and go away; and if it was a tiger then you shall go, and I will marry a new wife."

"As you like," answered the Queen; "there isn't any doubt which it was."

So the King called the two soldiers who were on guard outside and put the question to them. But, whilst the dispute was going on, the King and Queen had got so excited and talked so loud that the guards had heard nearly all they said, and one man observed to the other:

"Mind you declare that the King is right. It certainly was a jackal, but, if we say so, the King will probably not keep his word about going away, and we shall get into trouble, so we had better take his side."

To this the other agreed; therefore, when the King asked them what animal they had seen, both the guards said it was certainly a tiger, and that the King was right of course, as he always was. The King made no remark, but sent for a palanquin, and ordered the Queen to be placed in it, bidding the four bearers of the palanquin to take her a long way off into the forest and there leave her. In spite of her tears, she was forced to obey, and away the bearers went for three days and three nights until they came to a dense wood. There they set down the palanquin with the Queen in it, and started home again.

Now the Queen thought to herself that the King could not mean to send her away for good, and that as soon as he had got over his fit of temper he would summon her back; so she stayed quite still for a long time, listening with all her ears for approaching footsteps, but heard none. After a while she grew nervous, for she was all alone, and put her head out of the palanquin and looked about her. Day was just breaking, and birds and insects were beginning to stir; the leaves rustled in a warm breeze; but, although the queen's eyes wandered in all directions, there was no sign of any human being. Then her spirit gave way, and she began to cry.

It so happened that close to the spot where the Queen's palanquin had been set down, there dwelt a man who had a tiny farm in the midst of the forest, where he and his wife lived alone far from any neighbours. As it was hot weather the farmer had been sleeping on the flat roof of his house, but was awakened by the sound of weeping. He jumped up and ran downstairs as fast as he could, and into the forest towards the place the sound came from, and there he found the palanquin.

"Oh, poor soul that weeps," cried the farmer, standing

a little way off, "who are you?" At this salutation from a stranger the Queen grew silent, dreading she knew not what.

"Oh, you that weep," repeated the farmer, "fear not to speak to me, for you are to me as a daughter. Tell me, who are you?"

His voice was so kind that the Queen gathered up her courage and spoke. And when she had told her story, the farmer called his wife, who led her to their house, and gave her food to eat, and a bed to lie on. And in the farm, a few days later, a little prince was born, and by his mother's wish named Ameer Ali.

Years passed without a sign from the King. His wife might have been dead for all he seemed to care, though the Queen still lived with the farmer, and the little Prince had by this time grown up into a strong, handsome, and healthy youth. Out in the forest they seemed far from the world; very few ever came near them, and the Prince was continually begging his mother and the farmer to be allowed to go away and seek adventures and to make his own living. But she and the wise farmer always counselled him to wait, until, at last, when he was eighteen years of age, they had not the heart to forbid him any longer. So he started off one early morning, with a sword by his side, a big brass pot to hold water, a few pieces of silver, and a galail[1] in his hand, with which to shoot birds as he travelled.

Many a weary mile he tramped day after day, until, one morning, he saw before him just such a forest as that in which he had been born and bred, and he stepped joyfully

[1] A galail is a double-stringed bow from which bullets or pellets of hard dried clay can be fired with considerable force and precision.

into it, like one who goes to meet an old friend. Presently, as he made his way through a thicket, he saw a pigeon which he thought would make a good dinner, so he fired a pellet at it from his galail, but missed the pigeon, which fluttered away with a startled clatter. At the same instant he heard a great clamour from beyond the thicket, and, on reaching the spot, he found an ugly old woman streaming wet and crying loudly as she lifted from her head an earthen vessel with a hole in it from which the water was pouring. When she saw the Prince with his galail in his hand, she called out:

"Oh, wretched one! Why must you choose an old woman like me to play your pranks upon? Where am I to get a fresh pitcher instead of this one that you have broken with your foolish tricks? And how am I to go so far for water twice when one journey wearies me?"

"But, mother," replied the Prince, "I played no trick upon you! I did but shoot at a pigeon that should have served me for dinner, and as my pellet missed it, it must have broken your pitcher. But, in exchange, you shall have my brass pot, and that will not break easily; and as for getting water, tell me where to find it, and I'll fetch it while you dry your garments in the sun, and carry it whither you will."

At this the old woman's face brightened. She showed him where to seek the water, and when he returned a few minutes later with his pot filled to the brim, she led the way without a word, and he followed. In a short while they came to a hut in the forest, and as they drew near it Ameer Ali beheld in the doorway the loveliest damsel his eyes had ever looked on. At the sight of a stranger she drew her veil about her and stepped into the hut, and much as he wished to see her again Ameer Ali could think of no excuse by which to bring her back, and so, with a heavy heart, he made his salutation, and bade the old woman farewell. But when he had gone a little way she called after him:

"If ever you are in trouble or danger, come to where you now stand and cry: 'Fairy of the forest! Fairy of the forest, help me now!' And I will listen to you."

The Prince thanked her and continued his journey, but he thought little of the old woman's saying, and much of the lovely damsel. Shortly afterwards he arrived at a city; and, as he was now in great straits, having come to the end of his money, he walked straight to the palace of the King and asked for employment. The King said he had plenty of servants and wanted no more; but the young man pleaded so hard that at last the Rajah was sorry for him, and promised that he should enter his bodyguard on the condition that he would undertake any service which was especially difficult or dangerous. This was just what Ameer Ali wanted, and he agreed to do whatever the King might wish.

Soon after this, on a dark and stormy night, when the river roared beneath the palace walls, the sound of a woman weeping and wailing was heard above the storm. The King ordered a servant to go and see what was the matter; but the servant, falling on his knees in terror, begged that he might not be sent on such an errand, particularly on a night so wild, when evil spirits and witches were sure to be abroad. Indeed, so frightened was he, that the King, who was very kind-hearted, bade another go in his stead, but each one showed the same strange fear. Then Ameer Ali stepped forward:

"This is my duty, your Majesty," he said; "I will go."

The King nodded, and off he went. The night was as

dark as pitch, and the wind blew furiously and drove the rain in sheets into his face; but he made his way down to the ford under the palace walls and stepped into the flooded water. Inch by inch, and foot by foot he fought his way across, now nearly swept off his feet by some sudden swirl or eddy, now narrowly escaping being caught in the branches of some floating tree that came tossing and swinging down the stream.

At length he emerged, panting and dripping wet, on the other side. Close by the bank stood a gallows, and on the gallows hung the body of some evil-doer, whilst from the foot of it came the sound of sobbing that the King had heard.

Ameer Ali was so grieved for the one who wept there that he thought nothing of the wildness of the night or of the roaring river. As for ghosts and witches, they had never troubled him, so he walked up towards the gallows where crouched the figure of the woman.

"What ails you?" he said.

Now the woman was not really a woman at all, but a horrid kind of witch who really lived in Witchland, and had no business on earth. If ever a man strayed into Witchland the ogresses used to eat him up, and this old witch thought she would like to catch a man for supper, and that is why she had been sobbing and crying in hopes that someone out of pity might come to her rescue.

So when Ameer Ali questioned her, she replied:

"Ah, kind sir, it is my poor son who hangs upon that gallows; help me to get him down and I will bless you for ever."

Ameer Ali thought that her voice sounded rather eager than sorrowful, and he suspected that she was not telling the truth, so he determined to be very cautious.

"That will be rather difficult," he said, "for the gallows are high, and we have no ladder."

"Ah, but if you will just stoop down and let me climb upon your shoulders," answered the old witch, "I think I could reach him." And her voice now sounded so cruel that Ameer Ali was sure that she intended some evil. But he only said:

"Very well, we will try." With that he drew his sword, pretending that he needed it to lean upon, and bent so that the old woman could clamber on to his back, which she did very nimbly. Then, suddenly, he felt a noose slipped over his neck, and the old witch sprang from his shoulders on to the gallows, crying:

"Now, foolish one, I have got you, and will kill you for my supper."

But Ameer Ali gave a sweep upwards with his sharp sword to cut the rope that she had slipped round his neck, and not only cut the cord but cut also the old woman's foot as it dangled above him; and with a yell of pain and anger she vanished into the darkness.

Ameer Ali then sat down to collect himself a little, and felt upon the ground by his side an anklet that had evidently fallen off the old witch's foot. This he put into his pocket, and as the storm had by this time passed over he made his way back to the palace. When he had finished his story, he took the anklet out of his pocket and handed it to the King, who, like everyone else, was amazed at the glory of the jewels which composed it. Indeed, Ameer Ali himself was astonished, for he had slipped the anklet into his pocket in the dark and had not looked at it since. The king was delighted at its beauty, and having praised and rewarded Ameer Ali, he gave the anklet to his daughter, a proud and spoiled princess.

Now in the women's apartments in the palace there hung two cages, in one of which was a parrot and in the other a starling, and these two birds could talk as well as human beings. They were both pets of the Princess who always fed them herself, and the next day, as she was walking grandly about with her treasure tied round her ankle, she heard the starling say to the parrot:

"Oh, Toté," (that was the parrot's name) "how do you think the Princess looks in her new jewel?"

"Think?" snapped the parrot, who was cross because they hadn't given him his bath that morning, "I think she looks like a washerwoman's daughter, with one shoe on and the other off! Why doesn't she wear two of them, instead of going about with one leg adorned and the other bare?"

When the Princess heard this she burst into tears; and sending for her father she declared that he must get her another such an anklet to wear on the other leg, or she would die of shame.

So the King sent for Ameer Ali and told him that he must get a second anklet exactly like the first within a month, or he should be hanged, for the Princess would certainly die of disappointment.

Poor Ameer Ali was greatly troubled at the King's command, but he thought to himself that he had, at any rate, a month in which to lay his plans. He left the palace at once, and inquired of everyone where the finest jewels were to be got; but though he sought night and day he never found one to compare with the anklet. At last only a week remained, and he was in sore difficulty, when he remembered the Fairy of the forest, and determined to go without loss of time and seek her. Therefore away he went, and after a day's travelling he reached the cottage in the forest, and, standing where he had stood when the old woman called to him, he cried:

"Fairy of the forest! Fairy of the forest! Help me! Help me!"

Then there appeared in the doorway the beautiful girl he had seen before, whom in all his wanderings he had never forgotten.

"What is the matter?" she asked, in a voice so soft that he listened like one struck dumb, and she had to repeat the question before he could answer. Then he told her his story, and she went within the cottage and came back with two wands, and a pot of boiling water. The two wands she planted in the ground about six feet apart, and then, turning to him, she said:

"I am going to lie down between these two wands. You must then draw your sword and cut off my foot, and, as soon as you have done that, you must seize it and hold it over the cauldron, and every drop of blood that falls from it into the water will become a jewel. Next you must change the wands so that the one that stood at my head is at my feet, and the one at my feet stands at my head, and place the severed foot against the wound and it will heal, and I shall become quite well again as before."

At first Ameer Ali declared that he would sooner be hanged twenty times over than treat her so roughly; but at length she persuaded him to do her bidding. He nearly fainted himself with horror when he found that, after the cruel blow which lopped her foot off, she lay as one lifeless; but he held the severed foot over the cauldron, and, as drops of blood fell from it, and he saw each turn in the water into shining gems, his heart took courage. Very soon there were plenty of jewels in the cauldron, and he quickly changed the wands, placed the severed foot against the wound, and immediately the two parts became one as before. Then the maiden opened her eyes, sprang to her feet, and drawing her veil about her, ran into the hut, and would not come out or speak to him any more. For a long while he waited, but, as she did not appear, he gathered up the precious stones and returned to the palace. He easily got someone to set the jewels, and found that there were enough to make, not only one, but three rare and beautiful anklets, and these he duly presented to the King on the very day that his month of grace was over.

The King embraced him warmly, and made him rich gifts; and the next day the vain Princess put two anklets on each foot, and strutted up and down in them admiring herself in the mirrors that lined her room.

"Oh, Toté," asked the starling, "how do you think our Princess looks now in these fine jewels?"

"Ugh!" growled the parrot, who was really always cross in the mornings, and never recovered his temper until after lunch. "She's got all her beauty at one end of her now; if she had a few of those fine gew-gaws round her neck and wrists she would look better; but now, to my mind, she looks more than ever like the washerwoman's daughter dressed up."

Poor Princess! she wept and stormed and raved until she made herself quite ill; and then she declared to her father that unless she had bracelets and necklace to match the anklet she would die.

Again the King sent for Ameer Ali and ordered him to get a necklace and bracelets to match those anklets within a month, or be put to a cruel death.

And again Ameer Ali spent nearly the whole month searching for the jewels, but all in vain. At length he made his way to the hut in the forest, and stood and cried:

"Fairy of the forest! Fairy of the forest! Help me! Help me!"

Once more the beautiful maiden appeared at his summons and asked what he wanted, and when he had told her she said he must do exactly as he had done the first time, except that now he must cut off both her hands and her head. Her words turned Ameer Ali pale with horror; but she reminded him that no harm had come to her before, and at last he consented to do as she bade him. From her severed hands and head there fell into the cauldron bracelets and chains of rubies and diamonds, emeralds and pearls that surpassed any that ever were seen. Then the head and hands were joined on to the body, and left neither sign nor scar. Full of gratitude, Ameer Ali tried to speak to her, but she ran into the house and would not come back, and he was forced to leave her and go away laden with the jewels.

When, on the day appointed, Ameer Ali produced a necklace and bracelets each more beautiful and priceless than the last, the King's astonishment knew no bounds, and as for his daughter she was nearly mad with joy. The very next morning she put on all her finery, and thought that now, at least, that disagreeable parrot could find no fault with her appearance, and she listened eagerly when she heard the starling say:

"Oh, Toté, how do you think our Princess is looking *now*?"

"Very fine, no doubt," grumbled the parrot; "but what is the use of dressing up like that for oneself only? She ought to have a husband—why doesn't she marry the man who got her all these splendid things?"

Then the Princess sent for her father and told him that she wished to marry Ameer Ali.

"My dear child," said her father, "you really are very difficult to please, and want something new every day. It certainly is time you married someone, and if you choose this man, of course he shall marry you."

So the King sent for Ameer Ali, and told him that within a month he proposed to do him the honour of marrying him to the Princess, and making him heir to the throne.

On hearing this speech Ameer Ali bowed low and answered that he had done and would do the King all the service that lay in his power, save only this one thing. The King, who considered his daughter's hand a prize for any man, flew into a passion, and the Princess was more furious still. Ameer Ali was instantly thrown into the most dismal prison that they could find, and ordered to be kept there until the King had time to think in what way he should be put to death.

Meanwhile the King determined that the Princess ought in any case to be married without delay, so he sent forth heralds throughout the neighbouring countries, proclaiming that on a certain day any person fitted for a bridegroom and heir to the throne should present himself at the palace.

When the day came, all the court were gathered together, and a great crowd assembled of men, young and old, who thought that they had as good a chance as anyone else to gain both the throne and the Princess. As soon as the King was seated, he called upon an usher to summon the first claimant. But, just then, a farmer, who stood in front of the crowd, cried out that he had a petition to offer.

"Well, hasten then," said the King; "I have no time to waste."

"Your majesty," said the farmer, "has now lived and administered justice long in this city, and will know that the tiger who is king of beasts hunts only in the forest, whilst jackals hunt in every place where there is something to be picked up."

"What is all this? What is all this?" asked the King. "The man must be mad!"

"No, your majesty," answered the farmer; "I would only remind your majesty that there are plenty of jackals gathered today to try and claim your daughter and kingdom; every city has sent them, and they wait hungry and eager; but do not, O King, mistake or pretend again to mistake the howl of a jackal for the hunting cry of a tiger."

The king turned first red and then pale.

"There is," continued the farmer, "a royal tiger bred in the forest who has the first and only true claim to your throne."

"Where? What do you mean?" stammered the King, growing pale as he listened.

"In prison," replied the farmer; "if your majesty will clear this court of the jackals I will explain."

"Clear the court!" commanded the King; and, very unwillingly, the visitors left the palace.

"Now tell me what riddle this is," said he.

Then the farmer told the King and his ministers how he had rescued the Queen and brought up Ameer Ali; and he fetched the old Queen herself, whom he had left outside. At the sight of her the King was filled with shame and self-reproach, and wished he could have lived his life over again, and not have married the mother of the proud Princess, who caused him endless trouble until her death.

"My day is past," said he. And he gave up his crown to his son Ameer Ali, who went once more and called to the forest fairy to provide him with a queen to share his throne.

"There is only one person I will marry," said he. And this time the maiden did not run away, but agreed to be his wife. So the two were married without delay, and lived long and reigned happily.

As for the old woman whose pitcher Ameer Ali had broken, she was the forest maiden's fairy godmother, and when she was no longer needed to look after the girl she gladly returned to fairyland.

The old King has never been heard to contradict his wife any more. If he even looks as if he does not agree with her, she smiles at him and says:

"Is it the tiger, then, or the jackal?" And he has not another word to say.

Mother Goose had a Word for it

I

The Queen of Hearts
She made some tarts,
All on a summer's day;
The Knave of Hearts
He stole those tarts,
And took them clean away.

The King of Hearts
Called for the tarts,
And beat the knave full sore;
The Knave of Hearts
Brought back the tarts,
And vowed he'd steal no more.

2

Lavender's blue, diddle, diddle,
    Lavender's green;
When I am king, diddle, diddle,
    You shall be queen.

Who told you so, diddle, diddle,
    Who told you so?
'Twas my own heart, diddle, diddle,
    That told me so.

3

Lady Queen Anne she sits in the sun,
As fair as a lily, as white as a swan;
Come taste my lily, come smell my rose,
Which of my maidens do you choose?
The ball is ours and none of yours,
Go to the wood and gather flowers,
Cats and kittens now stay within,
While we young maidens walk out and in.

4

Pussy cat, pussy cat, where have you been?
I've been to London to visit the Queen.
Pussy cat, pussy cat, what did you there?
I frightened a little mouse under her chair.

The May Queen

A VICTORIAN LADY

You must wake and call me early, call me early, mother dear;
Tomorrow'll be the happiest time of all the glad New Year;
Of all the glad New Year, mother, the maddest merriest day;
For I'm to be Queen o' the May, mother, I'm to be Queen o' the May.

Queens of the May are less in the fashion than they were when Lord Tennyson wrote the poem of which some of us still know the first verse, and scarcely anybody ever knew the rest. In Queen Victoria's day when queens were all *the fashion, the prettiest girl in every village was chosen for the May Queen, and, crowned with flowers, ruled the country revels, where children danced round maypoles on village greens, and men danced along the roads with bells on their feet.*

In Bohemia, on the fourth Sunday in Lent, girls dressed in white with violets and daisies in their hair, led the Queen from door to door to announce the coming of spring, wish the inmates good luck, and receive presents; meanwhile her attendants had to keep whirling round and round, and must never stand still.

In Germany the Queen was crowned at Whitsuntide, and carried singing through the streets under a wreath like a tower. She too expected gifts from every house where her young attendants sang old ballads.

In the south of Ireland they crowned their Queen for the coming twelvemonth; she reigned over the dances and merrymakings all round the year. If she got married before the year ran out she lost her crown.

And in France—

But I can't do better here than tell you how they managed these things in France in the words of a Victorian English lady whose French mother took her little daughter on a visit to the South of France one spring a hundred years ago.

E.F.

The Victorian Lady's Tale

WHEN I was quite a child, I went with my mother to visit her relatives at a small town in the South of France.

We arrived about the end of April, when the spring had fully burst forth, with its deep blue sky, its balmy air, its grassy meadows, its flowering hedges and trees already green.

One morning I went out with my mother to call upon a friend: when we had taken a few steps down the street, she said:

"Today is the first of May; if the customs of my childhood are still preserved here, we shall see some 'Mays' on our road."

"Mays," I said, repeating a word I heard for the first time, "what are they?"

My mother replied by pointing to the opposite side of the place we were crossing.

"Stop, look there," she said; "that is a May."

Under the Gothic arch of an old church porch a narrow step was raised covered with palms. A living being, or a statue—I could not discern at the distance—dressed in a white robe, crowned with flowers, was seated upon it; in her right hand she held a leafy branch; a canopy above her head was formed of garlands of box, and ample draperies which fell on either side encircled her in their snowy folds.

No doubt the novelty of the sight caused my childish imagination much surprise, my eyes were captivated, and I scarcely listened to my mother, who gave me her ideas

on this local custom; ideas, the simple and sweet poetry of which I prefer to accept instead of discussing their original value.

"Because the month of May is the month of spring," said she, "the month of flowers, the month consecrated to the Virgin, the young girls of each *quartier* unite to celebrate its return. They choose a pretty child, and dress her as you see; they seat her on a throne of foliage, they crown her and make her a sort of goddess; she is May, the Virgin of May, the Virgin of lovely days, flowers, and green branches. See, they beg of the passers-by, saying, 'For the May.' People give, and their offerings will be used some of these days for a joyous festival."

When we came near, I recognized in the May a lovely little girl I had played with on the previous day. At a distance I thought she was a statue. Even close at hand the illusion was still possible; she seemed to me like a goddess on her pedestal, who neither distinguished nor recognized the profane crowd passing beneath her feet. Her only care was to wear a serene aspect under her crown of periwinkle and narcissus, laying her hand on her olive sceptre. She had, it is true, a gracious smile on her lips, a sweet expression in her eyes; but these, though charming all, did not seem to seek or speak to any in particular; they served as an adornment to her motionless physiognomy, lending life to the statue, but neither voice nor affections. Was it coquetry in so young a child thus studying to gain admiration? I know not, but to this day I can only think of the enchantment I felt in May.

My mother stopped, and drawing some money from her purse, laid it on the china saucer that was presented; as for myself, I took a handful of *sous*, all that I could find in my pocket, and gave them with transport; I was too young to appreciate the value of my gift, but I felt the exquisite pleasure of giving.

In passing through the town we met with several other "Mays", pretty little girls, perhaps, but not understanding their part; always restless, arranging their veils, touching their crowns, talking, eating sweetmeats, or weary, stiff, half asleep, or with an awkward, unpleasing attitude. None was the May, the representative of the season of sweet and lovely flowers, but my first little friend.

As I have seene the lady of the May
Set in an harbour
Built by the May-pole, where the jocund swains
Dance with the maidens to the bagpipe's straines,
When envious night commands them to be gone,
Call for their merry yongsters one by one,
And for their well performance some disposes,
To this a garland interwove with roses;
To that a carved hooke, or well wrought scrip;
Gracing another with her cherry lip:
To one her garter, to another then
A handkerchiefe cast o're and o're again;
And none returneth empty, that hath spent
His paynes to fill their rurall merriment.

From Browne's *Britannia's Pastorals*

Vashishta and the Four Queens

C. A. KINCAID

ONCE upon a time there was a town called Atpat. In it there ruled a king who had four wives. They were always quarrelling over the housework; so, in order to get some peace at home, the king himself divided the work between them. To the first queen he gave all the dairy work, to the second queen he gave all the cooking, to the third he gave the nursery, and he ordered the fourth queen to look after the royal wardrobe.

At first all went well. But in a little while the first queen said to the third queen, "Why should you have charge of the nursery? Why should you not work in the dairy?" The second queen said to the fourth queen, "Why should I have to do all the cooking?" The third queen asked, "Why should I have always to look after the children?" And the fourth queen stamped her foot and said, "I *won't* look after the king's clothes." And all day long they quarrelled and screamed at each other, and the poor king was more uncomfortable than ever. His face grew sad and care-worn, and, from the time he got up to the time he went to bed, he could think of nothing but the way that his four queens were squabbling with each other.

One day the rishi, or sage, Vashishta[1] paid the king a visit. The king prostrated himself before the great sage and gave him a throne to sit upon. Vashishta looked at the king's face and saw how sad and care-worn it was. He asked the cause, and the king told him. Then the rishi rose, and the king went with him to the palace of the four queens. When they reached it, they called to the queens to come out. The rishi then asked them why they quarrelled. The first queen cried out, "Why should I have to do the dairy work?" And the second queen cried out, "Why should I be only a cook-woman?" And the third cried out, "Why should I have all the children to look after?" And the fourth cried out, "Why should I have all the bother of sorting out all the king's clothes?" The king said, "You must do these things because I ordered you to." But the queens did not mind a word that he said, and they all screamed together so loud that the king and the rishi had to put their fingers in their ears to save themselves from being deafened. For a while the rishi became absorbed in thought, and then he turned to the first queen and said, "You have been placed in charge of the dairy, have you not?" The first queen assented. "Then listen to me," said Vashishta. "In a former life you were a cow, and near the spot in the jungle where you used to graze was an altar to Shiva. And every day at noon you used to come and stand near it and let milk drop upon it. And, because in this way you honoured the god Shiva, you have in this life become one of the queens of the king of Atpat. But you did not in your former life attain to full merit. So the god Shiva directed the king to place you in charge of his dairy, and

[1] Vashishta was the family priest of King Dasaratha, father of Ramchandra. After death he became one of the stars in the constellation of the Great Bear.

the king conveyed the god's directions to you. You should therefore obey them, and you should honour the king as if he were Shiva himself. In this way you will attain to full merit and ascend to Shiva's heaven, Kailas." Vashishta then blessed the first queen. She prostrated herself before him, and, giving up all thought of quarrelling, went away and busied herself with her dairy work.

Then Vashishta turned to the second queen and asked, "What are you quarrelling about?" She replied, "Why should I be just a cook-woman?" The rishi thought for a while and said, "Lady, in a former life you were the wife of a poor Brahman, and you used to beg your food from door to door. But every Monday you used to fast, and whatever grain you begged that day you used to cook and offer to the god Shiva. And he was pleased with your devotion. Therefore in this life he made you one of the queens of Atpat. And because you cooked for the god Shiva, he directed the king to put you in charge of his kitchen. Therefore, obey the god's directions and give a great feast to all in Atpat. In this way you will gain the favour of Shiva, and he will take you with him to Kailas." Then he blessed the second queen, and she prostrated herself and went off quite cheerfully to cook the king's dinner.

The sage next turned to the third queen and asked, "What are you quarrelling about?" The queen answered, "Why should I do nothing but fiddle about the nursery?" Vashishta thought for a while and said, "In a former life, O Queen, you were a maid of a jungle tribe. Every Monday you used to fast yourself and offer the choicest fruits that you picked to the god Shiva. In return for them he has made you a queen, and he has entrusted the king's children to you. Therefore look after them and be kind to them, and in the end he will take you to live with him in Kailas." The rishi then blessed the third queen, and she prostrated herself before him. Then she ran off, her face all smiles, to play with the king's children.

Vashishta last of all turned to the fourth queen and said, "What are you quarrelling about?" She answered, "Why should I do nothing but look after the king's clothes?" The rishi said, "In a former life, O Queen, you were a kite that flew high up in the heavens. Beneath where you used to fly was an altar to Shiva, and every day at noon you would spread your wings over it and shade it from the sun's heat. So the god was pleased with you and in this life made you one of the queens of Atpat. As you spread your wings over Shiva's altar, so now a canopy hangs over your bed. And just as you served Shiva, now do service to the king, your husband. And you will thereby gain full merit and in the end reach Kailas." Then the rishi blessed her, and she went off quite gaily to attend to the king's clothes.

And the four queens never quarrelled any more, but lived happily ever afterwards with the king. And all little girls who hear this story should try to be as good as the queens were after Vashishta had cured them of their squabbling.

Anne

1702–1714

ELEANOR AND HERBERT FARJEON

Queen Anne's dead!
Poor Queen Anne!
If she was plain
She had a pretty fan,
If she was dull,
She wore a pretty gown,
And almost looked alive
Underneath her crown.

Queen Anne's dead!
Poor plain Anne!
Fold her pretty gown,
Close her pretty fan,
And on her pretty monument
Let nothing else be read
But these plain words:
Queen Anne's dead!

The Miracle of the Poor Island

ELEANOR FARJEON

Eleanor Farjeon lives in a tiny cottage at the bottom of a cobbled lane in a village somewhere in London. I can sometimes get there, but at other times I get lost; or sometimes I find myself there when I was trying to get to a different place altogether. When I am there we talk, sometimes one at a time, sometimes both together, about the one hundred and twenty years we share between us—Eleanor is only eighty-four, so far. Then, when I'm leaving, she will say, "William, what about our book?" and I will say, "Eleanor, that is what I came to talk about. Didn't I mention it?" We might, you see, have been talking about tree-frogs, or Eleanor's grandmother's twenty-five sisters, or the ceiling. We talk about the ceiling quite a lot. Whatever it was, we start again. Then, when I leave, I walk downhill for a mile or two, and come out into the mortal world. Eleanor has a charitable cat called Benny who invites a friend home to tea if the friend looks hungry.

W.M.

P.S. I'm sorry, William, but I will not *let you whitewash my smoky ceiling. I know whitewash is fun for the one who's doing it, but you'd be the one. Then you'd go away, and I would be left staring up at glaring dead-white boards instead of the lovely cobwebby rafters of two hundred years ago, when this loft was full of hay instead of my books and me. That's how I like it. I'm sorry, William.*

E.F.

P.S. I am bad at painting, Eleanor, and I am sure the ceiling would still be interesting after I had finished. Of course I would paint round *the spiders—I never stroke other people's pets.*

W.M.

THE Queen had a Pleasure Island, a little out to sea. When she wanted to make merry, she sailed there from her palace on the mainland, in a gilded barque, with silk flags flying. Her Court accompanied her, there were musicians on deck too, and she came to her Pleasure Island amid flowers and music. There she spent her days picnicking and dancing under the trees. Everything that could make her island rich and prosperous was brought there in abundance from the mainland.

Farther out to sea lay a poor fishing-island. Here there was no abundance, and life was a hard battle. It was barren ground, stony or marshy, where grass scarcely grew, no trees or shrubs, and no flowers. Yes, there was just one flower, a small white rose-bush which belonged to little Lois. Her father's hut lay in the lee of the church that stood in the middle of the stony isle. He had scraped together a little soil, and the day he was married he brought the rose-tree over from the mainland, and set it by his door. His young bride tended it with so much care that it could not help growing; and when she died, Lois, who had known the rose as long as she had known her mother, tended it as her mother had done. It did not grow very big, its flowers were few, and sometimes bitten by the salt wind, but it was the only flower on the island, and the islanders were proud of it. Lois took care of it, but it seemed to belong to them all; it was the Island Flower.

Dangerous rocks surrounded the Poor Island, and its position exposed it to the roughest storms. Sometimes for days together the boats dared not put out from it, and those on the mainland could not approach it. The islanders were too poor to keep much store of food by them, nor could they grow it; so when the fishing-boats could not put out, the hard times were still harder. In fair weather the men lost no opportunity of getting fish. Most of it the women salted down for their own use; the rest they took to the mainland to sell for a little money, and they came back with flour and salt and materials to mend their nets with. But the men, who shared in common the few boats on which their trade depended, could hardly spare time to take their wives over and back, so the women waited till the tide went out. For there was in those parts an unusual tide, which once a month, at the full moon, receded far back into the ocean, leaving bare all the sand between the mainland and the island. The sea-bed lay exposed for a long time, long enough for the women to hurry over the sand with their creels of fish, and sell them to the merchants on the beach, and buy the few things that they needed most. Then the women trooped back across the patches of rock and stretches of ribbed sand, reaching the Poor Island just before the tide flowed in and cut them off. Sometimes they had to hurry, and had not time to complete their purchases, for they dared not be caught in the mouth of the rolling tide.

One evening, when the tide was out, the Queen looked from her Pleasure Island, and saw the band of women hurrying home. She had hardly noticed or thought of them before, but tonight the sight of them struck her heart. On the bare sand, where small pools gleamed with colours of the sunset, her own little isle lay like a glowing jewel; her summer palace, her gardens, fountains, and pavilions shone in the sun, and she herself, in her silk and silver gown, was like a Queen of Fairyland. While yonder, over the waste, the bare-legged women in their faded gowns, with their baskets on their backs, trudged to the Poor Island, which lay like a stone in the distance; not like a precious stone, but a common pebble. Yet perhaps, thought the Queen, there was something precious on it. "How sorrowful, how sorrowful to live on the Poor Island!" she thought. And suddenly she put her hand to her heart and sighed; for Queens have sorrows too, and perhaps even the poor folk had none greater than hers.

She looked across, and wondered; and little Lois standing far away on the Poor Island, looked across and wondered too. Even at that distance she could see the Pleasure Island like a jewel, she could see the small bright spires and domes and towers of the palace bathed in light, and on the breeze that blew towards her she could hear faint strains of music, and even smell sweet flowers. "How lovely, how lovely it must be to live on the Pleasure Island," thought Lois. And suddenly she stooped to smell her rose, for even the Queen, she thought, had no sweeter flower than this.

The Queen sent for her Chamberlain and said, "I wish to go and visit the Poor Island."

"That will be a new diversion for Your Majesty," said the Chamberlain. "When will you go?"

"The day after tomorrow," said the Queen.

Next day the Chamberlain sent word to the Poor Island that the Queen was coming. She had not intended him to do this, but he thought it fitting that the Islanders should have a chance to prepare for the honour that was to be bestowed upon them. An honour indeed they held it. Such a thing had never happened before. The Queen herself was coming! How could they welcome her? Where could they receive her?

"We will receive her in the church," said the Pastor.

And how could they entertain her? Should not the church be adorned for the Queen? The men and women met together to consult. They had nothing with which to adorn the church. There was the rose-bush, the Island Flower with its white blooms, but could they use that? No, said the father of Lois, if we do so we shall have nothing to show the Queen when she asks us, "And what is the most beautiful thing on your Island?" And now we can all take her to see the rose bush, and that will please her.

Little Lois was a-bed when the consultation was held. Her thoughts were full of the morrow and the coming of the Queen.

The day dawned, and the people gathered on the beach. The Pastor was with them, but Lois stayed behind to wipe the steps of the church porch, for it had rained in the night, and the step was spattered with mud. Then she started to run after the others, fearing she would be late, and as she did so—splash! she was ankle-deep in a big puddle right in the middle of the path. She looked with dismay at her wet feet, not that she cared for herself, but this was the way the Queen must walk, and the muddy place was too wide to step over. How could even the Poor Island let the Queen tread in the mud? And look, there was her golden barque coming over the water already. Something must be done quickly, for she would soon be here.

It was only after the Queen had come ashore that Lois joined the people on the beach. The Queen was talking to the Pastor, and kissing the children as he told her their names. Some of her courtiers were with her, and followed her up the rough road to the church. "What a God-forsaken place!" Lois heard one say to another, when their fine shoes stumbled on the stones. Her heart beat painfully as they approached the marshy spot which she had done her best to mend. Would her means hold good? Yes, the Queen passed over dry-foot.

Inside the Church the people stood up and sang. There

was no organ, but the Pastor gave the note, and they lifted their voices in a song of praise. When the song was over, the Pastor spoke a few words of thanksgiving to God who had sent the Queen to see them. Lois, who could not take her eyes off the Queen's beautiful face, saw that her eyes were as wet as the wet place on the ground, from which Lois had tried to protect her. But who can protect even a Queen from her tears?

When the people had sung one more song, they all went outside again. The Queen then said, "May I see your homes and how you live? Is living very hard here?"

The Pastor was about to answer, Yes, but the father of Lois stepped forward, and spoke with sturdy cheerfulness, "Life is hard everywhere, I take it," said he. "But no life is so hard that it has not something beautiful to show. And so it is with us on the Poor Island."

"What is your beautiful thing?" asked the Queen. "May I see it?"

"Gladly, madam. It is a rose-bush."

The folk pressed round her eagerly explaining, "Yes, madam, it is such a rose-bush as you never saw! White roses, madam! It is the Island's only flower. It is in bloom now, madam; there are nine roses on it, and three more coming. It is the Island's happiness, madam. Let us show it you, it is only a few steps just behind the church."

The poor folk bore the Queen around the corner, the fine folk following after. And when the proud excited crowd had reached the place, and the father of Lois led the Queen to his door to show her the rose-bush, there was nothing to see. Only a little scattered earth, where the rose-bush had been pulled up by the roots. The poor folk gasped, the courtiers tittered a little; and round the corner Lois knelt and wept. She wept beside the green leaves and white blossoms of her rose-bush, where she had strewn them that the Queen might not wet her feet.

The Queen sailed away in her golden barque, the visit was over, and life went on in the Poor Island as before. The Queen had gone away full of resolves. She would give an organ to the church, she would have good roads made, she would rebuild the poor huts, cartloads of soil should be carried over, and everyone should have a little garden. She would do all these things. Before she could do any of them, she died.

News reached the Poor Island that she had died suddenly of a secret pain; when she was buried, they buried her with the tears that had filled her heart and eyes in the Poor Island. No one else had shed these tears, they were her own; no one else, when she was dead, was concerned with their cause. Surely the Queen's tears were dried now. What had moved her to them was forgotten, what she had meant to do was left undone. Life went on in the Poor Island as before; only, it had lost its flower.

Nobody blamed Lois for what she had done. She had done right, they said; many of them would have done the same. When the Queen came to visit them, they could not let her walk in the wet, and now she was dead they were glad she had not had to do so. But Lois mourned; she mourned for her rose and for the Queen. To comfort her, her father promised her another rose, cost what it might.

The full moon came round again. Once more the sea ran back into itself, once more the women went in long procession to the mainland over the bared sand. This time the father of Lois went too, a hard-saved coin in his pocket. They sold their fish and made their purchases; and Lois' father bought a tiny rose-bush, another white one, which might with time become the Island's joy. While he was

making his bargain, one of the women ran and tapped him on the shoulder. "Come quick!" she said. "The sky looks threatening."

He looked at the sky and answered. "Yes, we must hasten. I only saw it look so once before, when the tide rushed in and took the women unawares."

All the women were flocking over the sand. The fisherman hurried after them; their one thought was to reach the Poor Island before the sea rushed in.

On the Island there was nobody but one or two girls, the children, and the Pastor. The men were out at sea on the other side. Those on the Island saw the darkening sky, and felt the breath in the air that presaged danger. They came down to watch for the return of the women. Lois came too, straining her eyes for her father. Far off on the dark wet stretch of sand the children saw their mothers coming like little ants—they were already far from the mainland, and they still had far to come. Then, swiftly, what all feared most took place. The tide rushed in and surrounded the Poor Island; and it surged on, with waves that raced each other like wild horses, on towards the little band of people in the distance. There was no hope, no help, no refuge. Before they could turn back, the tide must take them.

The Pastor knelt upon the rocks and prayed, and all the children knelt with him, praying and crying. Only Lois stood upright among them, gazing. For the deserted Pleasure Island of the Queen was streaming with pale light, that no one except Lois seemed to see; and in the light the Queen herself was standing. Distant as she was, like someone in a dream, Lois saw her as plainly as she had seen her in the church, when the people were singing; but her eyes were wet no longer, and a lovely smile was on her face. She was smiling straight at Lois, and in her

hands were nine white roses with their green leaves. And as the wild green waves with their white caps rolled to the very feet of the Poor Islanders, the Queen cast leaves and flowers upon the water. The tide rolled on, covering all the space between the islands. But oh wonder! it was

covered not with the green-and-white sea, but with a heap of green leaves and white flowers. The tide of roses reached from isle to isle, and on it the women walked dry-foot to their children, and Lois' father came safe with her new tree.

The people talk of the miracle to this day. If you do not believe it, go to the Poor Island for yourself, where the rose is growing still.

The Billy Goat and the King

ANDREW LANG

This story is from the Olive Fairy Tale Book *of Andrew Lang. Editors of books like this one have to use stories from Lang, because he bagged them all long ago—and what a good thing, or we shouldn't know them.*

W.M.

ONCE there lived a certain King who understood the language of all birds and beasts and insects. This knowledge had of course been given him by a fairy godmother; but it was rather a troublesome present, for he knew that if he were ever to reveal anything he had thus learned he would turn into a stone. How he managed to avoid doing so long before this story opens I cannot say, but he had safely grown up to manhood, and married a wife, and was as happy as monarchs generally are.

This King, I must tell you, was a Hindu; and when a Hindu eats his food he has a nice little place on the ground, freshly plastered with mud, and he sits in the middle of it with very few clothes on—which is quite a different way from ours.

Well, one day the King was eating his dinner in just such a nice, clean, mud-plastered spot, and his wife was

sitting opposite to wait upon him and keep him company. As he ate he dropped some grains of rice upon the ground, and a little ant, who was running about seeking a living, seized upon one of the grains and bore it off towards his hole. Just outside the King's circle this ant met another ant, and the King heard the second one say:

"Oh, dear friend, do give me that grain of rice, and get another one for yourself. You see my boots are so dirty that, if I were to go upon the King's eating place, I should defile it, and I can't do that, it would be so very rude."

But the owner of the grain of rice only replied:

"If you want rice go and get it. No one will notice your dirty boots; and you don't suppose that I am going to carry rice for all our kindred?"

Then the King laughed.

The Queen looked at herself up and down, but she could not see or feel anything in her appearance to make the King laugh, so she said:

"What are you laughing at?"

"Did I laugh?" replied the King.

"Of course you did," retorted the Queen; "and if you think that I am ridiculous I wish you would say so, instead of behaving in that stupid way! What are you laughing at?"

"I'm not laughing at anything," answered the King.

"Very well, but you *did* laugh, and I want to know why."

"Well, I'm afraid I can't tell you," said the King.

"You *must* tell me," replied the Queen impatiently. "If you laugh when there's nothing to laugh at you must be ill or mad. What is the matter?"

Still the King refused to say, and still the Queen declared that she must and would know. For days the quarrel went on, and the Queen gave her husband no rest, until at last the poor man was almost out of his wits, and thought that, as life had become for him hardly worth living while this went on, he might as well tell her the secret and take the consequences.

"But," thought he, "if I am to become a stone, I am not going to lie, if I can help it, on some dusty highway, to be kicked here and there by man and beast, flung at dogs, be used as the plaything of naughty children, and become generally restless and miserable. I will be a stone at the bottom of the cool river, and roll gently about there until I find some secure resting-place where I can stay for ever."

So he told his wife that if she would ride with him to

the middle of the river he would tell her what he had laughed at. She thought he was joking, and laughingly agreed; their horses were ordered and they set out.

On the way they came to a fine well beneath the shade of some lofty, wide-spreading trees, and the King proposed that they should get off and rest a little, drink some of the cool water, and then pass on. To this the Queen consented; so they dismounted and sat down in the shade by the well-side to rest.

It happened that an old goat and his wife were browsing in the neighbourhood, and, as the King and Queen sat there, the nanny goat came to the well's brink and peering over saw some lovely green leaves that sprang in tender shoots out of the side of the well.

"Oh!" cried she to her husband, "come quickly and look. Here are some leaves which make my mouth water; come and get them for me!"

Then the billy goat sauntered up and looked over, and after that he eyed his wife a little crossly.

"You expect me to get you those leaves, do you? I suppose you don't consider how in the world I am to reach them? You don't seem to think at all; if you did you would know that if I tried to reach those leaves I should fall into the well and be drowned!"

"Oh," cried the nanny goat, "why should you fall in? Do try and get them!"

"I am not going to be so silly," replied the billy goat.

But the nanny goat still wept and entreated.

"Look here," said her husband, "there are plenty of fools in the world, but I am not one of them. This silly King here, because he can't cure his wife of asking questions, is going to throw his life away. But I know how to cure you of your follies, and I'm going to."

And with that he butted the nanny goat so severely that in two minutes she was submissively feeding somewhere else, and had made up her mind that the leaves in the well were not worth having.

Then the King, who had understood every word, laughed once more.

The Queen looked at him suspiciously, but the King got up and walked across to where she sat.

"Are you still determined to find out what I was laughing at the other day?" he asked.

"Quite," answered the Queen angrily.

"Because," said the King, tapping his leg with his riding whip, "I've made up my mind not to tell you, and moreover, I have made up my mind to stop you mentioning the subject any more."

"What *do* you mean?" asked the Queen nervously.

"Well," replied the King, "I notice that if that goat is displeased with his wife, he just butts her, and that seems to settle the question—"

"Do you mean to say you would *beat* me!" cried the Queen.

"I should be extremely sorry to have to do so," replied the King; "but I have to persuade you to go home quietly, and to ask no more silly questions when I say I cannot answer them. Of course, if you *will* persist, why—"

And the Queen went home, and so did the King; and it is said that they are both happier and wiser than ever before.

The Marriage of Queen Magdalen

FROM CHAMBERS "BOOK OF DAYS"

IN the summer of 1536 the young Scottish monarch, James V, voyaged to France to see the daughter of the Duc de Vendôme with a view to marriage; but not affecting her on intimate acquaintance, he turned his thoughts to the royal family as likely to furnish him a better bride. The king, Francis I, received him with great kindness at a place to the south of Lyons, and thence conducted him to a castle where his family was residing. He found the Princess Magdalen unable to ride on horseback, as her mother and other ladies did, but obliged by weakness of health to be carried in a chariot.

Yet, not withstanding her sickness—so the Scottish historian Lindsay informs us—*fra the time she saw the king of Scotland and spak with him, she became so enamoured of him, and loved him so weel, that she wold have no man alive to her husband but he enarly* (only).

Sage counsellors of both countries discommended the union; but the young princess easily induced her father to consent, and the consent of the King, his father, followed. On the 1st of January the pair were united in the church of Notre Dame, in the presence of seven cardinals and a

great assemblage of the French nobility, amidst circumstances of great pomp and popular joy.

Through all France that day, there was jousting and running of horse proclaimed, with all other manly exercise; as also skirmishing of ships through all the coasts; so that in towns, lands, seas, firths, castles, and towers, there was no man that might have heard for the raird (uproar) *and noise of cannons, nor scarcely have seen for the vapours thereof. There was also within the town of Paris, cunning carvers and profound necromancers, who by their art caused things appear whilk wes not, as follows: fowls flying in the air spouting fire on others, rivers of water running through the town and ships fechtand* (fighting) *therupon.*

With his young bride, and a hundred thousand crowns by way of dowry, gifted moreover with twenty-war-horses, as many suits of elegant mail, two great war-ships, and a vast quantity of jewels and other articles, the young Scottish monarch set sail for his own country. Landing at Leith on Whit Sunday, the young queen, full of love for her husband and his country, knelt on the shore, took up a handful of sand and kissed it, invoking God's blessing upon Scotland. She was received in Edinburgh with triumphs and shows of unexampled grandeur, with, what was far better, the affectionate reverence of the entire people. But the doom had already been passed upon her. She withered like an uprooted flower, and only forty days from her arrival, lay a corpse in her husband's palace.

The death of this beautiful young creature in such interesting circumstances, made a deep impression on the national heart, and it is understood to have been the first occasion of a general mourning being assumed in Scotland.

Circe's Palace

NATHANIEL HAWTHORNE

Nathaniel Hawthorne lived just over a hundred years ago. In reading this story you will notice that there is not a great deal of difference between the way he writes and the way writers write now, although the times are so far apart. Hawthorne was an American, and he didn't copy anyone else. In his time he was very modern, and other writers are only just catching up with him, which is why he still reads so well. He would have been an uncomfortable neighbour. In fact, he had to leave his own town, Salem, and live somewhere else, because people began to recognize themselves in his books. They didn't like it, because he was truthful about them (who would?). The trouble was that his neighbours at that time thought they were naturally perfect, and Hawthorne disagreed and said why.

Meanwhile, here is a story about an ancient queen. (I don't think this is the story the people of Salem saw themselves in.)

W.M.

SOME of you have heard, no doubt, of the wise King Ulysses, and how he went to the siege of Troy, and how, after that famous city was taken and burned, he spent ten long years in trying to get back again to his own little kingdom of Ithaca. At one time in the course of this weary voyage, he arrived at an island that looked very green and pleasant, but the name of which was unknown to him. For, only a little while before he came thither, he had met with a terrible hurricane, or rather a great many hurricanes at once, which drove his fleet of vessels into a strange part of the sea, where neither himself nor any of his mariners had ever sailed. This misfortune was entirely owing to the foolish curiosity of his shipmates, who, while Ulysses lay asleep, had untied some very bulky leathern bags, in which they supposed a valuable treasure to be concealed. But in each of these stout bags, King Aeolus, the ruler of the winds, had tied up a tempest, and had given it to Ulysses to keep, in order that he might be sure of a favourable passage homeward to Ithaca; and when the strings were loosened, forth rushed the whistling blasts, like air out of a blown bladder, whitening the sea with foam, and scattering the vessels nobody could tell whither.

Immediately after escaping from this peril a still greater one had befallen him. Scudding before the hurricane, he reached a place, which, as he afterwards found, was called Laestrygonia, where some monstrous giants had eaten up many of his companions, and had sunk every one of his vessels, except that in which he himself sailed, by flinging great masses of rock at them from the cliffs along the shore. After going through such troubles as these, you cannot wonder that King Ulysses was glad to moor his tempest-beaten bark in a quiet cove of the green island, which I began with telling you about. But he had encountered so many dangers from giants, and one-eyed Cyclops, and monsters of the sea and land, that he could not help dreading some mischief, even in this pleasant and seemingly solitary spot. For two days, therefore, the poor weatherworn voyagers kept quiet, and either stayed on board their vessel, or merely crept along under the cliffs that bordered the shore; and to keep themselves alive, they dug shell-fish out of the sand, and sought for any little rill of fresh water that might be running towards the sea.

Before the two days were spent, they grew very weary of this kind of life; for the followers of King Ulysses, as you will find it important to remember, were terrible gormandizers, and pretty sure to grumble if they missed their regular meals, and their irregular ones besides. Their stock of provisions was quite exhausted, and even the shell-fish began to get scarce, so that they had now to choose between starving to death or venturing into the interior of the island, where perhaps some huge three-headed dragon, or other horrible monster, had his den. Such misshapen creatures were very numerous in those days; and nobody ever expected to make a voyage, or take a journey, without running more or less risk of being devoured by them.

But King Ulysses was a bold man as well as a prudent one; and on the third morning he determined to discover what sort of a place the island was, and whether it were possible to obtain a supply of food for the hungry mouths of his companions. So, taking a spear in his hand, he clambered to the summit of a cliff, and gazed round about him. At a distance, towards the centre of the island, he beheld the stately towers of what seemed to be a palace, built of snow-white marble, and rising in the midst of a grove of lofty trees. The thick branches of these trees stretched across the front of the edifice, and more than half concealed it, although, from the portion which he saw, Ulysses judged it to be spacious and exceedingly beautiful, and probably the residence of some great nobleman or prince. A blue smoke went curling up from a chimney, and was almost the pleasantest part of the spectacle to Ulysses. For, from the abundance of this smoke, it was reasonable to conclude that there was a good fire in the kitchen, and that, at dinner-time, a plentiful banquet would be served up to the inhabitants of the palace, and to whatever guests might happen to drop in.

With so agreeable a prospect before him, Ulysses fancied that he could not do better than to go straight to the palace gate, and tell the master of it that there was a crew of poor shipwrecked mariners, not far off, who had eaten nothing for a day or two save a few clams and oysters, and would therefore be thankful for a little food. And the prince or nobleman must be a very stingy curmudgeon, to be sure, if at least, when his own dinner was over, he would not bid them welcome to the broken victuals from the table.

Pleasing himself with this idea, King Ulysses had made a few steps in the direction of the palace, when there was a great twittering and chirping from the branch of a neighbouring tree. A moment afterwards, a bird came flying towards him, and hovered in the air, so as almost to brush his face with its wings. It was a very pretty little bird, with purple wings and body, and yellow legs, and a circle of golden feathers round its neck, and on its head a golden tuft, which looked like a king's crown in miniature. Ulysses tried to catch the bird. But it fluttered nimbly out of his reach, still chirping in a piteous tone, as if it could have told a lamentable story, had it only been gifted with human language. And when he attempted to drive it away, the bird flew no further than the bough of the next tree, and again came fluttering about his head, with its doleful chirp, as soon as he showed a purpose of going forward.

"Have you anything to tell me, little bird?" asked Ulysses.

And he was ready to listen attentively to whatever the

bird might communicate; for at the siege of Troy, and elsewhere, he had known such odd things to happen, that he would not have considered it much out of the common run had this little feathered creature talked as plainly as himself.

"Peep!" said the bird, "peep, peep, pe—weep!" And nothing else would it say, but only, "Peep, peep, pe—weep!" in a melancholy cadence, and over and over and over again. As often as Ulysses moved forward, however, the bird showed the greatest alarm, and did its best to drive him back, with the anxious flutter of its purple wings. Its unaccountable behaviour made him conclude, at last, that the bird knew of some danger that awaited him, and which must needs be very terrible, beyond all question, since it moved even a little fowl to feel compassion for a human being. So he resolved, for the present, to return to the vessel, and tell his companions what he had seen.

This appeared to satisfy the bird. As soon as Ulysses turned his back, it ran up the trunk of a tree, and began to pick insects out of the bark with its long, sharp bill; for it was a kind of woodpecker, you must know, and had to get its living in the same manner as other birds of that species. But every little while, as it pecked at the bark of the tree, the purple bird bethought itself of some secret sorrow, and repeated its plaintive note of "Peep, peep, pe—weep!"

On his way to the shore, Ulysses had the good luck to kill a large stag by thrusting his spear into its back. Taking it on his shoulders (for he was a remarkably strong man) he lugged it along with him, and flung it down before his hungry companions. I have already hinted to you what gormandizers some of the comrades of King Ulysses were. From what is related of them, I reckon that their favourite

diet was pork, and that they had lived upon it until a good part of their physical substance was swine's flesh; and their tempers and dispositions were very much akin to the hog. A dish of venison, however, was no unacceptable meal to them, especially after feeding so long on oysters and clams. So, beholding the dead stag, they felt of its ribs, in a knowing way, and lost no time in kindling a fire of driftwood to cook it. The rest of the day was spent in feasting, and if these enormous eaters got up from the table at sunset, it was only because they could not scrape another morsel off the poor animal's bones.

The next morning their appetites were as sharp as ever. They looked at Ulysses, as if they expected him to clamber up the cliff again, and come back with another fat deer upon his shoulders. Instead of setting out, however, he summoned the whole crew together, and told them it was in vain to hope that he could kill a stag every day for their dinner, and therefore it was advisable to think of some other mode of satisfying their hunger.

"Now," said he, "when I was on the cliff yesterday, I discovered that this island is inhabited. At a considerable distance from the shore stood a marble palace, which appeared to be very spacious, and had a great deal of smoke curling out of one of its chimneys."

"But," continued the wise Ulysses, "you must remember, my good friends, our misadventure in the cavern of one-eyed Polyphemus, the Cyclops! Instead of his ordinary milk diet, did he not eat up two of our comrades for his supper, and a couple more for breakfast, and two at his supper again? Methinks I see him yet, the hideous monster, scanning us with that great red eye, in the middle of his forehead, to single out the fattest. And then, again, only a few days ago, did we not fall into the hands of the king of the Laestrygons, and those other horrible giants, his subjects, who devoured a great many more of us than are now left? To tell you the truth, if we go to yonder palace, there can be no question that we shall make our appearance at the dinner-table; but whether seated as guests, or served up as food, is a point to be seriously considered."

"Either way," murmured some of the hungriest of the crew, "it will be better than starvation, particularly if one could be sure of being well fattened beforehand, and daintily cooked afterwards."

"That is a matter of taste," said King Ulysses, and, "for my own part, neither the most careful fattening nor the daintiest of cookery would reconcile me to being dished at last. My proposal is, therefore, that we divide ourselves into two equal parties, and ascertain, by drawing lots, which of the two shall go to the palace, and beg for food and assistance. If these can be obtained, all is well. If not, and if the inhabitants prove as inhospitable as Polyphemus, or the Laestrygons, then there will but half of us perish, and the remainder may set sail and escape."

As nobody objected to this scheme, Ulysses proceeded to count the whole band, and found that there were forty-six men including himself. He then numbered off twenty-two of them, and put Eurylochus (who was one of his chief officers, and second only to himself in sagacity) at their head. Ulysses took command of the remaining twenty-two men, in person. Then, taking off his helmet, he put two shells into it, on one of which was written, "Go," and on the other "Stay". Another person now held the helmet, while Ulysses and Eurylochus drew out each a shell; and the word "Go" was found written on that which Eurylochus had drawn. In this manner, it was decided that Ulysses and his twenty-two men were to remain at the seaside until the other party should have found out what sort of treatment they might expect at the mysterious palace. As there was no help for it, Eurylochus immediately set forth at the head of his twenty-two followers, who went off in a very melancholy state of mind, leaving their friends in hardly better spirits than themselves.

No sooner had they clambered up the cliff, than they discerned the tall marble towers of the palace, ascending, as white as snow, out of the lovely green shadow of the trees which surrounded it. A gush of smoke came from a chimney in the rear of the edifice. The vapour rose high in the air, and, meeting with a breeze, was wafted seaward, and made to pass over the heads of the hungry mariners. When people's appetites are keen, they have a very quick scent for anything savoury in the wind.

"That smoke comes from the kitchen!" cried one of them, turning up his nose as high as he could, and snuffing eagerly. "And, as sure as I'm a half-starved vagabond, I smell roast meat in it."

"Pig, roast pig!" said another. "Ah, the dainty little porker! My mouth waters for him."

"Let us make haste," cried the others, "or we shall be too late for the good cheer!"

But scarcely had they made half a dozen steps from the edge of the cliff when a bird came fluttering to meet them. It was the same pretty little bird, with the purple wings and body, the yellow legs, the golden collar round its neck, and the crown-like tuft upon its head, whose behaviour had so much surprised Ulysses. It hovered about Eurylochus, and almost brushed his face with its wings.

"Peep, peep, pe—weep!" chirped the bird.

So plaintively intelligent was the sound, that it seemed

as if the little creature were going to break its heart with some mighty secret that it had to tell, and only this one poor note to tell it with.

"My pretty bird," said Eurylochus—for he was a wary person, and let no token of harm escape his notice—"my pretty bird, who sent you hither? And what is the message which you bring?"

"Peep, peep, pe—weep!" replied the bird, very sorrowfully.

Then it flew towards the edge of the cliff, and looked round at them, as if exceedingly anxious that they should return whence they came. Eurylochus and a few of the others were inclined to turn back. They could not help suspecting that the purple bird must be aware of something mischievous that would befall them at the palace, and the knowledge of which affected its airy spirit with a human sympathy and sorrow. But the rest of the voyagers, snuffing up the smoke from the palace kitchen, ridiculed the idea of returning to the vessel. One of them (more brutal than his fellows, and the most notorious gormandizer in the whole crew) said such a cruel and wicked thing, that I wonder the mere thought did not turn him into a wild beast, in shape, as he already was in his nature.

"This troublesome and impertinent little fowl," said he, "would make a delicate titbit to begin dinner with. Just one plump morsel, melting away between the teeth. If he comes within my reach, I'll catch him, and give him to the palace cook to be roasted on a skewer."

The words were hardly out of his mouth, before the purple bird flew away, crying, "Peep, peep, pe—weep!" more dolorously than ever.

"That bird," remarked Eurylochus, "knows more than we do about what awaits us at the palace."

"Come on, then," cried his comrades, "and we'll soon know as much as he does."

The party, accordingly, went onward through the green and pleasant wood. Every little while they caught new glimpses of the marble palace, which looked more and more beautiful the nearer they approached it. They soon entered a broad pathway which seemed to be very neatly kept, and which went winding along with streaks of sunshine falling across it, and specks of light quivering among the deepest shadows that fell from the lofty trees. It was bordered, too, with a great many sweet-smelling flowers, such as the mariners had never seen before. So rich and beautiful they were, that, if the shrubs grew wild here, and were native in the soil, then this island was surely the flower garden of the whole earth; or, if transplanted from some other clime, it must have been from the Happy Islands that lay towards the golden sunset.

"There has been a great deal of pains foolishly wasted on these flowers," observed one of the company; and I tell you what he said, that you may keep in mind what gormandizers they were. "For my part, if I were the owner of the palace, I would bid my gardener cultivate nothing but savoury pot-herbs to make a stuffing for roast meat, or to flavour a stew with."

"Well said!" cried the others. "But I'll warrant you there's a kitchen garden in the rear of the palace."

At one place they came to a crystal spring, and paused to drink at it for want of liquor which they liked better. Looking into its bosom, they beheld their own faces dimly reflected, but so extravagantly distorted by the gush and motion of the water, that each of them appeared to be laughing at himself and all his companions. So ridiculous were these images of themselves, indeed, that they did really laugh aloud, and could hardly be grave again as soon as they wished. And after they had drank, they grew still merrier than before.

"It has a twang of a wine cask in it," said one, smacking his lips.

"Make haste!" cried his fellows; "we'll find the wine cask itself at the palace; and that will be better than a hundred crystal fountains."

Then they quickened their pace, and capered for joy at the thought of the savoury banquet at which they hoped to be guests. But Eurylochus told them that he felt as if he were walking in a dream.

"If I am really awake," continued he, "then, in my opinion, we are on the point of meeting with some stranger adventure than any that befell us in the cave of Polyphemus, or among the gigantic man-eating Laestrygons, or in the windy palace of King Aeolus, which stands on a brazen-walled island. This kind of dreamy feeling always comes over me before any wonderful occurrence. If you take my advice, you will turn back."

"No, no," answered his comrades, snuffing the air, in which the scent from the palace kitchen was now very perceptible. "We would not turn back, though we were certain that the king of the Laestrygons, as big as a mountain, would sit at the head of the table, and huge Polyphemus, the one-eyed Cyclops, at its foot."

At length they came within full sight of the palace, which proved to be very large and lofty, with a great number of airy pinnacles upon its roof. Though it was now midday, and the sun shone brightly over the marble front, yet its snowy whiteness, and its fantastic style of architecture, made it look unreal, like the frostwork on a window pane, or like the shapes of castles which one sees among the clouds by moonlight. But, just then, a puff of wind brought down the smoke of the kitchen chimney among them, and caused each man to smell the odour of the dish that he liked best; and, after scenting it, they thought everything else moonshine, and nothing real save this palace, and save the banquet that was evidently ready to be served up in it.

So they hastened their steps towards the portal, but had not got half-way across the wide lawn, when a pack of lions, tigers, and wolves came bounding to meet them. The terrified mariners started back, expecting no better fate than to be torn to pieces and devoured. To their surprise and joy, however, these wild beasts merely capered around them, wagging their tails, offering their heads to be stroked and patted, and behaving just like so many well-bred house dogs, when they wish to express their delight at meeting their master or their master's friends. The biggest lion licked the feet of Eurylochus; and every other lion, and every wolf and tiger, singled out one of his two and twenty followers, whom the beast fondled as if he loved him better than a beef bone.

But, for all that, Eurylochus imagined that he saw something fierce and savage in their eyes; nor would he have been surprised, at any moment, to feel the big lion's terrible claws, or to see each of the tigers make a deadly spring, or each wolf leap at the throat of the man whom he had fondled. Their mildness seemed unreal, and a mere freak; but their savage nature was as true as their teeth and claws.

Nevertheless, the men went safely across the lawn with the wild beasts frisking about them, and doing no manner of harm; although, as they mounted the steps of the palace, you might possibly have heard a low growl, particularly from the wolves; as if they thought it a pity, after all, to let the strangers pass without so much as tasting what they were made of.

Eurylochus and his followers now passed under a lofty portal, and looked through the open doorway into the interior of the palace. The first thing that they saw was a spacious hall, and a fountain in the middle of it, gushing up towards the ceiling out of a marble basin, and falling back into it with a continual splash. The water of this fountain, as it spouted upward, was constantly taking new shapes, not very distinctly, but plainly enough for a nimble fancy to recognize what they were. Now it was the shape of a man in a long robe, the fleecy whiteness of which was made out of the fountain's spray; now it was a lion, or a tiger, or a wolf, or an ass, or, as often as anything else, a hog, wallowing in the marble basin as if it were his sty. It was either magic or some very curious machinery that caused the gushing waterspout to assume all these forms. But, before the strangers had time to look closely at this wonderful sight, their attention was drawn off by a very sweet and agreeable sound. A woman's voice was singing melodiously in another room of the palace, and with her voice was mingled the noise of a loom, at which she was probably seated, weaving a rich texture of cloth, and intertwining the high and low sweetness of her voice into a rich tissue of harmony.

By and by, the song came to an end, and then, all at once, there were several feminine voices, talking airily and cheerfully, with now and then a merry burst of laughter such as you may always hear when three or four young women sit at work together.

"What a sweet song that was!" exclaimed one of the voyagers.

"Too sweet, indeed," answered Eurylochus, shaking his head. "Yet it was not so sweet as the song of the Sirens, those birdlike damsels who wanted to tempt us on the rocks, so that our vessel might be wrecked, and our bones left whitening along the shore."

"But just listen to the pleasant voices of those maidens, and the buzz of the loom, as the shuttle passes to and fro," said another comrade. "What a domestic, household, homelike sound it is! Ah, before that weary siege of Troy, I used to hear the buzzing loom and the women's voices under my own roof. Shall I never hear them again? Nor taste those nice little savoury dishes which my dearest wife knew how to serve up?"

"Tush! we shall fare better here," said another. "But how innocently those women are babbling together, without guessing that we overhear them! And mark that richest voice of all, so pleasant and familiar, but which yet seems to have the authority of a mistress among them. Let us show ourselves at once. What harm can the lady of the palace and her maidens do to mariners and warriors like us?"

"Remember," said Eurylochus, "that it was a young maiden who beguiled three of our friends into the palace of the king of the Laestrygons, who ate up one of them in the twinkling of an eye."

No warning or persuasion, however, had any effect on his companions. They went up to a pair of folding doors at the further end of the hall, and throwing them wide open, passed into the next room. Eurylochus, meanwhile, had stepped behind a pillar. In the short moment while the folding doors opened and closed again, he caught a glimpse of a very beautiful woman rising from the loom, and coming to meet the poor weatherbeaten wanderers, with a hospitable smile, and her hand stretched out in welcome. There were four other young women, who joined their hands and danced merrily forward, making gestures of obeisance to the strangers. They were only less beautiful than the lady who seemed to be their mistress. Yet Eurylochus fancied that one of them had sea-green hair, and that the close-fitting bodice of a second looked like the bark of a tree, and that both the others had something odd in their aspect, although he could not quite determine what it was, in the little while that he had to examine them.

The folding doors swung quickly back, and left him standing behind the pillar, in the solitude of the outer hall. There Eurylochus waited until he was quite weary, and listened eagerly to every sound, but without hearing anything that could help him to guess what had become of his friends. Footsteps, it is true, seemed to be passing and repassing in other parts of the palace. Then there was a clatter of silver dishes, or golden ones, which made him imagine a rich feast in a splendid banqueting hall. But by and by he heard a tremendous grunting and squealing, and then a sudden scampering, like that of small, hard hoofs over a marble floor, while the voices of the mistress and her four handmaidens were screaming altogether, in tones of anger and derision. Eurylochus could not conceive what had happened, unless a drove of swine had broken into the palace, attracted by the smell of the feast. Chancing to cast his eyes at the fountain, he saw that it did not shift its shape, as formerly, nor looked either like a long-robed man, or a lion, a tiger, a wolf, or an ass. It looked like nothing but a hog, which lay wallowing in the marble basin, and filled it from brim to brim.

But we must leave the prudent Eurylochus waiting in

the outer hall, and follow his friends into the inner secrecy of the palace. As soon as the beautiful woman saw them she arose from the loom, as I have told you, and came forward smiling, and stretching out her hand. She took the hand of the foremost among them, and bade him and the whole party welcome.

"You have been long expected, my good friends," said she. "I and my maidens are well acquainted with you, although you do not appear to recognize us. Look at this piece of tapestry, and judge if your faces must not have been familiar to us."

So the voyagers examined the web of cloth which the beautiful woman had been weaving in her loom; and, to their vast astonishment they saw their own figures perfectly represented in different coloured threads. It was a life-like picture of their recent adventures, showing them in the cave of Polyphemus, and how they had put out his one great moony eye; while in another part of the tapestry they were untying the leathern bags, puffed out with contrary winds; and further on, they beheld themselves scampering away from the gigantic king of the Laestrygons, who had caught one of them by the leg. Lastly, there they were, sitting on the desolate shore of this very island, hungry and downcast, and looking ruefully at the bare bones of the stag which they devoured yesterday. This was as far as the work had yet proceeded; but when the beautiful woman should again sit down at her loom, she would probably make a picture of what had since happened to the strangers, and of what was now going to happen.

"You see," she said, "that I know all about your troubles; and you cannot doubt that I desire to make you happy for as long a time as you may remain with me. For this purpose, my honoured guests, I have ordered a banquet to be prepared. Fish, fowl, and flesh, roasted and in luscious stews, and seasoned, I trust, to all your tastes, are ready to be served up. If your appetites tell you it is dinner-time, then come with me to the festal saloon."

At this kind invitation, the hungry mariners were quite overjoyed; and one of them, taking upon himself to be spokesman, assured their hospitable hostess that any hour of the day was dinner-time with them, whenever they could get flesh to put in the pot, and fire to boil it with. So the beautiful woman led the way; and the four maidens (one of them had sea-green hair, another a bodice of oak bark, a third sprinkled a shower of waterdrops from her fingers' ends, and the fourth had some other oddity which I have forgotten), all these followed behind, and hurried the guests along, until they entered a magnificent saloon. It was built in a perfect oval, and lighted from a crystal dome above. Around the walls were ranged two and twenty thrones, overhung by canopies of crimson and gold, and provided with the softest of cushions, which were tasselled and fringed with gold cord. Each of the strangers were invited to sit down; and there they were, two and twenty storm-beaten mariners in worn and tattered garb, sitting on two and twenty cushioned and canopied thrones, so rich and gorgeous that the proudest monarch had nothing more splendid in his stateliest hall.

Then you might have seen the guests nodding, winking with one eye, and leaning from one throne to another, to communicate their satisfaction in hoarse whispers.

"Our good hostess has made kings of us all," said one. "Ha! do you smell the feast? I'll engage it will be fit to set before two and twenty kings."

"I hope," said another, "it will be mainly good

substantial joints, sirloins, spareribs, and hinder quarters, without too many kickshaws. If I thought the good lady would not take it amiss, I should call for a fat slice of fried bacon to begin with."

Ah, the gluttons and gormandizers! You see how it was with them. In the loftiest seats of dignity, on royal thrones, they could think of nothing but their greedy appetite, which was the portion of their nature that they shared with wolves and swine; so that they resembled those vilest of animals far more than they did kings—if, indeed, kings were what they ought to be.

But the beautiful woman now clapped her hands; and immediately there entered a train of two and twenty serving-men, bringing dishes of the richest food, all hot from the kitchen fire, and sending up such a steam that it hung like a cloud below the crystal dome of the saloon. An equal number of attendants brought great flagons of wine, of various kinds, some of which sparkled as it was poured out, and went bubbling down the throat; while, of other sorts, the purple liquor was so clear that you could see the wrought figures at the bottom of the goblet. While the servants supplied the two and twenty guests with food and drink, the hostess and her four maidens went from one throne to another, exhorting them to eat their fill, and to quaff wine abundantly, and thus to recompense themselves, at this one banquet, for the many days when they had gone without a dinner. But, whenever the mariners were not looking at them (which was pretty often, as they looked chiefly into the basins and platters), the beautiful woman and her damsels turned aside and laughed. Even the servants, as they knelt down to present the dishes, might be seen to grin and sneer, while the guests were helping themselves to the offered dainties.

And, once in a while, the strangers seemed to taste something that they did not like.

"Here is an odd kind of a spice in this dish," said one. "I can't say it quite suits my palate. Down it goes, however."

"Send a good draught of wine down your throat," said his comrade on the next throne. "That is the stuff to make this sort of cookery relish well. Though I must needs say, the wine has a queer taste too. But the more I think of it the better I like the flavour."

Whatever little fault they might find with the dishes, they sat at dinner a prodigiously long while; and it would really have made you ashamed to see how they swilled down the liquor and gobbled up the food. They sat on golden thrones, to be sure, but they behaved like pigs in a sty; and, if they had had their wits about them, they might have guessed that this was the opinion of their beautiful hostess and her maidens. It brings a blush into my face to reckon up, in my own mind, what mountains of meat and pudding, and what gallons of wine, these two and twenty guzzlers and gormandizers ate and drank. They forgot all about their homes, and their wives and children, and all about Ulysses, and everything else, except this banquet, at which they wanted to keep feasting for ever. But at length they began to give over, from mere incapacity to hold any more.

"That last bit of fat is too much for me," said one.

"And I have not room for another morsel," said his next neighbour, heaving a sigh. "What a pity! My appetite is as sharp as ever."

In short, they all left off eating, and leaned back on their thrones, with such a stupid and helpless aspect as made them ridiculous to behold. When their hostess saw this she laughed aloud; so did her four damsels; so did the two and twenty serving-men that bore the dishes, and their two and twenty fellows that poured out the wine. And the louder they all laughed the more stupid and helpless did the two and twenty gormandizers look. Then the beautiful woman took her stand in the middle of the saloon, and stretching out a slender rod (it had been all the while in her hand, although they never noticed it till this moment) she turned it from one guest to another until each had felt it pointed at himself. Beautiful as her face was, and though there was a smile on it, it looked just as wicked and mischievous as the ugliest serpent that ever was seen; and fat-witted as the voyagers had made themselves, they began to suspect that they had fallen into the power of an evil-minded enchantress.

"Wretches," cried she, "you have abused a lady's hospitality, and in this princely saloon your behaviour has been suited to a hog-pen. You are already swine in everything but the human form, which you disgrace, and which I myself should be ashamed to keep a moment longer, were you to share it with me. But it will require only the slightest exercise of magic to make the exterior conform to the hoggish disposition. Assume your proper shapes, gormandizers, and begone to the sty!"

Uttering these last words, she waved her wand: and stamping her foot imperiously, each of the guests was struck aghast at beholding, instead of his comrades in human shape, one and twenty hogs sitting on the same number of golden thrones. Each man (as he still supposed himself to be) essayed to give a cry of surprise, but found that he could merely grunt, and that, in a word, he was just such another beast as his companions. It looked so intolerably absurd to see hogs on cushioned thrones, that they made haste to wallow down upon all fours like other swine. They tried to groan and beg for mercy, but forthwith emitted the most awful grunting and squealing that ever came out of swinish throats. They would have wrung their hands in despair, but, attempting to do so, grew all the more desperate for seeing themselves squatted on their hams, and pawing the air with their fore-trotters. Dear me!

what pendulous ears they had! what little red eyes, half buried in fat! and what long snouts, instead of Grecian noses!

But brutes as they certainly were, they yet had enough of human nature in them to be shocked at their own hideousness; and, still intending to groan, they uttered a viler grunt and squeal than before. So harsh and ear-piercing it was, that you would have fancied a butcher was sticking his knife into each of their throats, or, at the very least, that somebody was pulling every hog by his funny little twist of a tail.

"Begone to your sty!" cried the enchantress, giving them some smart strokes with her wand; and then she turned to the serving-men: "Drive out these swine, and throw down some acorns for them to eat."

The door of the saloon being flung open, the drove of hogs ran in all directions save the right one, in accordance with their hoggish perversity, but were finally driven into the back-yard of the palace. It was a sight to bring tears into one's eyes (and I hope none of you will be cruel enough to laugh at it) to see the poor creatures go snuffing along, picking up here a cabbage leaf and there a turnip-top, and rooting their noses in the earth for whatever they could find. In their sty, moreover, they behaved more piggishly than the pigs that had been born so; for they bit and snorted at one another, put their feet in the trough, and gobbled up their victuals in a ridiculous hurry and, when there was nothing more to be had, they made a great pile of themselves among some unclean straw, and fell fast asleep. If they had any human reason left, it was just enough to keep them wondering when they should be slaughtered and what quality of bacon they should make.

Meantime, as I told you before, Eurylochus had waited, and waited, and waited in the entrance hall of the palace, without being able to comprehend what had befallen his friends.

At last, when the swinish uproar resounded through the palace, and when he saw the image of a hog in the marble basin, he thought it best to hasten back to the vessel and inform the wise Ulysses of these marvellous occurrences. So he ran as fast as he could down the steps, and never stopped to draw breath till he reached the shore.

"Why do you come alone?" asked King Ulysses as soon

as he saw him. "Where are your two and twenty comrades?"

At these questions Eurylochus burst into tears. "Alas!" cried he, "I greatly fear that we shall never see one of their faces again."

Then he told Ulysses all that had happened, as far as he knew it, and added that he suspected the beautiful woman to be a vile enchantress, and the marble palace, magnificent as it looked, to be only a dismal cavern in reality. As for his companions, he could not imagine what had become of them, unless they had been given to the swine to be devoured alive. At this intelligence, all the voyagers were greatly affrighted. But Ulysses lost no time in girding on his sword, and hanging his bow and quiver over his shoulders, and taking a spear in his right hand. When his followers saw their wise leader making these preparations, they inquired whither he was going, and earnestly besought him not to leave them.

"You are our king," cried they, "and what is more, you are the wisest man in the whole world, and nothing but your wisdom and courage can get us out of this danger. If you desert us, and go to the enchanted palace, you will suffer the same fate as our poor companions, and not a soul of us will ever see our dear Ithaca again."

"As I am your king," answered Ulysses, "and wiser than any of you, it is therefore the more my duty to see what has befallen our comrades, and whether anything can yet be done to rescue them. Wait for me here until tomorrow. If I do not return, you must hoist sail and endeavour to find your way to our native land. For my part, I am answerable for the fate of these poor mariners, who have stood by my side in battle, and been so often drenched to the skin, along with me, by the same tempestuous surges. I will either bring them back with me or perish."

Had his followers dared, they would have detained him by force. But King Ulysses frowned sternly on them and shook his spear, and bade them stop him at their peril. Seeing him so determined, they let him go, and sat down on the sand, as disconsolate a set of people as could be, waiting and praying for his return.

It happened to Ulysses, just as before, that, when he had gone a few steps from the edge of the cliff, the purple bird came fluttering towards him, crying "Peep, peep, pe—weep!" and using all the art it could to persuade him to go no further.

"What mean you, little bird?" cried Ulysses. "You are arrayed like a king in purple and gold, and wear a golden crown upon your head. Is it because I too am a king that you desire so earnestly to speak with me? If you can talk in human language, say what you would have me do."

"Peep!" answered the purple bird, very dolorously. "Peep, peep, pe—we—ep!"

Certainly there lay some heavy anguish at the little bird's heart; and it was a sorrowful predicament that it could not, at least, have the consolation of telling what it was. But Ulysses had no time to waste in trying to get at the mystery. He therefore quickened his pace, and had gone a good way along the pleasant wood path, when there met him a young man of very brisk and intelligent aspect and clad in a rather singular garb. He wore a short cloak, and a sort of cap that seemed to be furnished with a pair of wings; and from the lightness of his step you would have supposed that there might likewise be wings on his feet. To enable him to walk still better (for he was always on one journey or another) he carried a winged staff, around which two serpents were wriggling and twisting. In short, I have said enough to make you guess that it was Quicksilver; and Ulysses (who knew him of old, and had learned a great deal of his wisdom from him) recognized him in a moment.

"Whither are you going in such a hurry, wise Ulysses?" asked Quicksilver. "Do you not know that this island is enchanted? The wicked enchantress (whose name is Circe, the sister of King Aeetes) dwells in the marble palace which you see yonder among the trees. By her magic arts, she changes every human being into the brute beast or fowl whom he happens most to resemble."

"That little bird, which met me at the edge of the cliff," exclaimed Ulysses; "was he a human being once?"

"Yes," answered Quicksilver. "He was once a king, named Picus, and a pretty good sort of a king too, only rather too proud of his purple robe, and his crown, and the golden chain about his neck; so he was forced to take the shape of a gaudy-feathered bird. The lions, and wolves, and tigers, who will come running to meet you, in front of the palace, were formerly fierce and cruel men, resembling in their disposition the wild beasts whose forms they now rightfully wear."

"And my poor companions," said Ulysses. "Have they undergone a similar change, through the arts of this wicked Circe?"

"You well know what gormandizers they were," replied Quicksilver; and, rogue that he was, he could not help laughing at the joke. "So you will not be surprised to hear that they have all taken the shapes of swine! If Circe had never done anything worse, I really should not think her so very much to blame."

"But can I do nothing to help them?" inquired Ulysses.

"It will require all your wisdom," said Quicksilver, "and a little of my own into the bargain, to keep your royal and sagacious self from being transformed into a fox. But do as I bid you; and the matter may end better than it has begun."

While he was speaking Quicksilver seemed to be in search of something; he went stooping along the ground, and soon laid his hand on a little plant with a snow-white flower, which he plucked and smelt of. Ulysses had been looking at that very spot only just before; and it appeared to him that the plant had burst into full flower the instant when Quicksilver touched it with his fingers.

"Take this flower, King Ulysses," said he. "Guard it as you do your eyesight, for I can assure you it is exceedingly rare and precious, and you might seek the whole earth over without ever finding another like it. Keep it in your hand, and smell of it frequently after you enter the palace, and while you are talking with the enchantress. Especially when she offers you food or a draught of wine out of her goblet, be careful to fill your nostrils with the flower's fragrance. Follow these directions, and you may defy her magic arts to change you into a fox."

Quicksilver then gave him some further advice how to behave, and bidding him be bold and prudent, again assured him that, powerful as Circe was, he would have fair prospect of coming safely out of her enchanted palace. After listening attentively, Ulysses thanked his good friend and resumed his way. But he had taken only a few steps, when, recollecting some other questions which he wished to ask, he turned round again, and beheld nobody on the spot where Quicksilver had stood; for that winged cap of his, and those winged shoes, with the help of the winged staff, had carried him quickly out of sight.

When Ulysses reached the lawn, in front of the palace, the lions and other savage animals came bounding to meet him, and would have fawned upon him and licked his feet. But the wise king struck at them with his long spear, and sternly bade them begone out of his path; for he knew that they had once been bloodthirsty men, and would now tear him limb from limb, instead of fawning upon him, could they do the mischief that was in their hearts. The wild beasts yelped and glared at him, and stood at a distance while he ascended the palace steps.

On entering the hall, Ulysses saw the magic fountain in the centre of it. The up-gushing water had now again taken the shape of a man in a long, white, fleecy robe, who appeared to be making gestures of welcome. The king likewise heard the noise of the shuttle in the loom, and the sweet melody of the beautiful woman's song, and then the pleasant voices of herself and the four maidens talking together, with peals of merry laughter intermixed. But Ulysses did not waste much time in listening to the laughter or the song. He leaned his spear against one of the pillars in the hall, and then, after loosening his sword in the scabbard, stepped boldly forward, and threw the folding doors wide open. The moment she beheld his stately figure standing in the doorway, the beautiful woman rose from the loom, and ran to meet him with a glad smile throwing its sunshine over her face, and both her hands extended.

"Welcome, brave stranger!" cried she. "We were expecting you."

And the nymph with the sea-green hair made a curtsy down to the ground, and likewise bade him welcome; so did her sister with the bodice of oaken bark, and she that sprinkled dew-drops from her fingers' ends, and the fourth one with some oddity which I cannot remember. And Circe, as the beautiful enchantress was called (who had deluded so many persons that she did not doubt of being able to delude Ulysses, not imagining how wise he was), again addressed him:

"Your companions," said she, "have already been received into my palace, and have enjoyed the hospitable treatment to which the propriety of their behaviour so well entitles them. If such be your pleasure, you shall first take some refreshment, and then join them in the elegant apartments which they now occupy. See, I and my maidens have been weaving their figures into this piece of tapestry."

She pointed to the web of beautifully woven cloth in the loom. Circe and the four nymphs must have been very diligently at work since the arrival of the mariners, for a great many yards of tapestry had now been wrought, in addition to what I before described. In this new part, Ulysses saw his two and twenty friends represented as sitting on cushioned and canopied thrones, greedily devouring dainties and quaffing deep draughts of wine. The work had not yet gone any further. Oh, no indeed. The enchantress was far too cunning to let Ulysses see the mischief which her magic arts had since brought upon the gormandizers.

"As for yourself, valiant sir," said Circe, "judging by the dignity of your aspect, I take you to be nothing less than a king. Deign to follow me, and you shall be treated as befits your rank."

So Ulysses followed her into the oval saloon, where his two and twenty comrades had devoured the banquet, which ended so disastrously for themselves, but all this while he had held the snow-white flower in his hand, and had constantly smelt of it while Circe was speaking; and as he crossed the threshold of the saloon, he took good care to inhale several long and deep snuffs of its fragrance. Instead of two and twenty thrones, which had before been ranged around the wall, there was now only a single throne in the centre of the apartment. But this was surely the most magnificent seat that ever a king or an emperor reposed himself upon, all made of chased gold, studded with precious stones, with a cushion that looked like a soft heap of living roses, and overhung by a canopy of sunlight which Circe knew how to weave into drapery. The enchantress took Ulysses by the hand, and made him sit down upon this dazzling throne. Then, clapping her hands, she summoned the chief butler.

"Bring hither," said she, "the goblet that is set apart for kings to drink out of. And fill it with the same delicious wine which my royal brother, King Aeetes, praised so highly, when he last visited me with my fair daughter Medea. That good and amiable child! Were she now here, it would delight her to see me offering this wine to my honoured guest."

But Ulysses, while the butler was gone for the wine, held the snow-white flower to his nose.

"Is it a wholesome wine?" he asked.

At this the four maidens tittered; whereupon the enchantress looked round at them with an aspect of severity.

"It is the wholesomest juice that ever was squeezed out of the grape," said she; "for, instead of disguising a man, as other liquor is apt to do, it brings him to his true self, and shows him as he ought to be."

The chief butler liked nothing better than to see people turned into swine, or making any kind of a beast of themselves; so he made haste to bring the royal goblet, filled with a liquid as bright as gold, and which kept sparkling upward, and throwing a sunny spray over the brim. But, delightful as the wine looked, it was mingled with the most potent enchantments that Circe knew how to concoct. For every drop of the pure grape-juice there were two drops of the pure mischief; and the danger of the thing was, that the mischief made it taste all the better. The mere smell of the bubbles, which effervesced at the brim, was enough to turn a man's beard into a pig's bristles, or make a lion's claws grow out of his fingers, or a fox's brush behind him.

"Drink, my noble guest," said Circe, smiling as she presented him with the goblet. "You will find in this draught a solace for all your troubles."

King Ulysses took the goblet with his right hand, while with his left he held the snow-white flower to his nostrils, and drew in so long a breath that his lungs were filled with its pure and simple fragrance. Then, drinking off all the wine, he looked the enchantress calmly in the face.

"Wretch," cried Circe, giving him a smart stroke with her wand, "how dare you keep your human shape a moment longer? Take the form of the brute whom you most resemble. If a hog, go join your fellow swine in the sty; if a lion, a wolf, a tiger, go howl with the wild beasts on the lawn; if a fox, go exercise your craft in stealing poultry. Thou hast quaffed off my wine, and canst be man no longer."

But, such was the virtue of the snow-white flower, instead of wallowing down from his throne in swinish shape, or taking any other brutal form, Ulysses looked even more manly and king-like than before. He gave the magic goblet a toss, and sent it clashing over the marble floor, to the furthest end of the saloon. Then, drawing his

sword, he seized the enchantress by her beautiful ringlets, and made a gesture as if he meant to strike off her head at one blow.

"Wicked Circe," cried he, in a terrible voice, "this sword shall put an end to thy enchantments. Thou shalt die, vile wretch, and do no more mischief in the world by tempting human beings into the vices which make beasts of them."

The tone and countenance of Ulysses were so awful, and his sword gleamed so brightly, and seemed to have so intolerably keen an edge, that Circe was almost killed by the mere fright, without waiting for a blow. The chief butler scrambled out of the saloon, picking up the golden goblet as he went, and the enchantress and the four maidens fell on their knees, wringing their hands, and screaming for mercy.

"Spare me!" cried Circe. "Spare me, royal and wise Ulysses. For now I know that thou art he of whom Quicksilver forewarned me, the most prudent of mortals, against whom no enchantments can prevail. Thou only couldst have conquered Circe. Spare me, wisest of men. I will show thee true hospitality, and even give myself to be thy slave, and this magnificent palace to be henceforth thy home."

The four nymphs, meanwhile, were making a most piteous ado; and especially the ocean nymph, with the sea-green hair, wept a great deal of salt water, and the fountain nymph, besides scattering dew-drops from her fingers' ends, nearly melted away into tears. But Ulysses would not be pacified until Circe had taken a solemn oath to change back his companions, and as many others as he should direct, from their present forms of beast or bird into their former shapes of men.

"On these conditions," said he, "I consent to spare your life. Otherwise you must die on the spot."

With a drawn sword hanging over her, the enchantress would readily have consented to do as much good as she had hitherto done mischief, however little she might like such employment. She therefore led Ulysses out of the back entrance of the palace, and showed him the swine in their sty. There were about fifty of these unclean beasts in the whole herd; and though the greater part were hogs by birth and education, there was wonderfully little difference to be seen betwixt them and their new brethren who had so recently worn the human shape. To speak critically, indeed, the latter rather carried the thing to excess, and seemed to make it a point to wallow in the miriest point of the sty, and otherwise to outdo the original swine in their own natural vocation. When men once turn to brutes, the trifle of man's wit that remains in them adds tenfold to their brutality.

The comrades of Ulysses, however, had not quite lost the remembrance of having formerly stood erect. When he approached the sty, two and twenty enormous swine separated themselves from the herd and scampered towards him, with such a chorus of horrible squealing as made him clap both hands to his ears. And yet they did not seem to know what they wanted, nor whether they were merely hungry, or miserable from some other cause. It was curious, in the midst of their distress, to observe them thrusting their noses into the mire, in quest of something to eat. The nymph with the bodice of oaken bark (she was the hamadryad of an oak) threw a handful of acorns among them; and the two and twenty hogs scrambled and fought for the prize, as if they had tasted not so much as a noggin of sour milk for a twelvemonth.

"These must certainly be my comrades," said Ulysses. "I recognize their disposition. They are hardly worth the trouble of changing them into the human form again. Nevertheless, we will have it done, lest their bad example should corrupt the other hogs. Let them take their original shapes, therefore, Dame Circe, if your skill is equal to the task. It will require greater magic, I trow, than it did to make swine of them."

So Circe waved her wand again, and repeated a few magic words, at the sound of which the two and twenty hogs pricked up their pendulous ears. It was a wonder to behold how their snouts grew shorter and shorter, and their mouths (which they seemed to be sorry for, because they could not gobble so expeditiously) smaller and smaller, and how one and another began to stand upon his hind legs, and scratch his nose with his fore-trotters. At first the spectators hardly knew whether to call them hogs or men, but by and by came to the conclusion that they rather resembled the latter. Finally, there stood the twenty-two comrades of Ulysses, looking pretty much the same as when they left the vessel.

You must not imagine, however, that the swinish quality had entirely gone out of them. When once it fastens itself into a person's character, it is very difficult getting rid of it. This was proved by the hamadryad, who, being exceedingly fond of mischief, threw another handful of acorns before the twenty-two newly restored people; whereupon down they wallowed, in a moment, and gobbled them up in a very shameful way. Then, recollecting themselves, they scrambled to their feet, and looked more than commonly foolish.

"Thanks, noble Ulysses!" they cried. "From brute beasts you have restored us to the condition of men again."

"Do not put yourselves to the trouble of thanking me," said the wise king. "I fear I have done but little for you."

To say the truth, there was a suspicious kind of grunt in their voices, and for a long time afterwards they spoke gruffly, and were apt to set up a squeal.

"It must depend upon your own future behaviour," added Ulysses, "whether you do not find your way back to the sty."

At this moment, the note of a bird sounded from the branch of a neighbouring tree.

"Peep, peep, pe—wee—ep!"

It was the purple bird, who, all this while, had been sitting over their heads, watching what was going forward, and hoping that Ulysses would remember how he had done his utmost to keep him and his followers out of harm's way. Ulysses ordered Circe instantly to make a king of this good little fowl, and leave him exactly as she found him. Hardly were the words spoken, and before the bird had time to utter another "Pe—weep," King Picus leaped down from the bough of the tree, as majestic a sovereign as any in the world, dressed in a long purple robe and gorgeous yellow stockings, with a splendidly wrought collar about his neck, and a golden crown upon his head. He and King Ulysses exchanged with one another the courtesies which belong to their elevated rank. But from that time forth, King Picus was no longer proud of his crown and his trappings of royalty, nor of the fact of his being a king; he felt himself merely the upper servant of his people, and that it must be his lifelong labour to make them better and happier.

As for the lions, tigers, and wolves (though Circe would have restored them to their former shapes at his slightest word), Ulysses thought it advisable that they should remain as they now were, and thus give warning of their cruel dispositions, instead of going about under the guise of men, and pretending to human sympathies, while their hearts had the bloodthirstiness of wild beasts. So he let them howl as much as they liked, but never troubled his head about them. And, when everything was settled according to his pleasure, he sent to summon the remainder of his comrades, whom he had left at the sea-shore. These being arrived, with the prudent Eurylochus at their head, they all made themselves comfortable in Circe's enchanted palace, until quite rested and refreshed from the toils and hardships of their voyage.

Henry and Mary

ROBERT GRAVES

Henry was a young king,
Mary was his queen;
He gave her a snowdrop
On a stalk of green.

Then all for his kindness
And for all his care,
She gave him a new-laid egg
In the garden there.

"Love, can you sing?"
"I cannot sing."
"Or tell a tale?"
"Not one I know."
"Then let us play at queen and king
As down the garden walks we go."

Snow-drop

GRIMM

Snow-drop *is Snow White, and it is from the great collection known as Grimm's Fairy Tales. Who was Grimm? Grimm was two people, Jacob and Wilhelm, the brothers Grimm. They were born about a year apart, and spent their lives together. As children they were inseparable, at the University they studied and lived together, as scholars they worked in the same room, and they were buried side by side in Berlin. The Fairy Tales were not their only work, but were among their favourite tasks. They lived on Grammar, and wrote books about it a thousand pages thick. They were interested in such things as finding out that ordinary English words like* fire, water, father, *or* egg *(for instance) were very nearly the same as the Indian words for the same things. In the end they found out why, and that is what the thousand pages were about. They found out, at the same time, that many different countries had the same stories. They were Germans, and this is a German story; but perhaps there is an Indian Snow White as well. We have put the story in because of the wicked queen, not really because of Snow White, or* Snow-drop.

W.M.

IT was in the middle of winter, when the broad flakes of snow were falling around, that a certain Queen sat working at a window the frame of which was made of fine black ebony; and as she was looking out upon the snow, she pricked her finger, and three drops of blood fell upon it. Then she gazed thoughtfully upon the red drops which sprinkled the white snow, and said, "Would that my little daughter may be as white as that snow, as red as the blood, and as black as the ebony window-frame!"

And so the little girl grew up: her skin was as white as snow, her cheeks as rosy as the blood, and her hair as black as ebony; and she was called Snow-drop.

But this Queen died; and the King soon married another wife, who was very beautiful, but so proud that she could not bear to think that anyone could surpass her. She had a magical looking-glass, to which she used to go and gaze upon herself in it, and say:

"Tell me, glass, tell me true!
Of all the ladies in the land
Who is the fairest? tell me who?"

And the glass answered:

"Thou, Queen, art fairest in the land."

But Snow-drop grew more and more beautiful; and when she was seven years old, she was as bright as the day, and fairer than the Queen herself. Then the glass one day answered the Queen when she went to consult it as usual:

"Thou, Queen, mays't fair and beauteous be,
But Snow-drop is lovelier far than thee!"

When she heard this she turned pale with rage and envy; and called to one of her servants and said, "Take Snow-drop away into the wide wood, that I may never see her more." Then the servant led her away; but his heart melted when she begged him to spare her life, and he said, "I will not hurt thee, thou pretty child." So he left her by herself; and though he thought it most likely that the wild beasts would tear her in pieces, he felt as if a great weight were taken off his heart when he had made up his mind not to kill her, but leave her to her fate.

Then poor Snow-drop wandered along through the wood in great fear; and the wild beasts roared about her,

but none did her any harm. In the evening she came to a little cottage, and went in there to rest herself, for her little feet would carry her no farther. Everything was spruce and neat in the cottage: on the table was spread a white cloth, and there were seven little plates with seven little loaves, and seven little glasses with wine in them; and knives and forks laid in order; and by the wall stood seven little beds. Then, as she was very hungry, she picked a little piece off each loaf, and drank a very little wine out of each glass; and after that she thought she would lie down and rest. So she tried all the little beds; and one was too long, and another was too short, till at last the seventh suited her; and there she laid herself down and went to sleep. Presently in came the masters of the cottage, who were seven little dwarfs that lived among the mountains, and dug and searched about for gold. They lighted up their seven lamps, and saw directly that all was not right. The first said, "Who has been sitting on my stool?" The second, "Who has been eating off my plate?" The third, "Who has been picking my bread?" The fourth, "Who has been meddling with my spoon?" The fifth, "Who has been handling my fork?" The sixth, "Who has been cutting with my knife?" The seventh, "Who has been drinking my wine?" Then the first looked round and said, "Who has been lying on my bed?" And the rest came running to him, and every one cried out that somebody had been upon his bed. But the seventh saw Snow-drop, and called all his brethren to come and see her; and they cried out with wonder and astonishment, and brought their lamps to look at her and said, "Good heavens! what a lovely child she is!" And they were delighted to see her, and took care not to wake her; and the seventh dwarf slept an hour with each of the other dwarfs in turn, till the night was gone.

In the morning Snow-drop told them all her story; and they pitied her, and said if she would keep all things in order, and cook and wash, and knit and spin for them, she might stay where she was, and they would take good care of her. Then they went out all day long to their work, seeking for gold and silver in the mountains; and Snow-drop remained at home; and they warned her, and said,

"The Queen will soon find out where you are, so take care and let no one in."

But the Queen, now that she thought Snow-drop was dead, believed that she was certainly the handsomest lady in the land; and she went to the glass and said:

"Tell me, glass, tell me true!
Of all the ladies in the land,
Who is fairest? tell me who?"

And the glass answered:

"Thou, Queen, art the fairest in all this land,
But over the hills, in the greenwood shade,
Where the seven dwarfs their dwelling have made,
There Snow-drop is hiding her head; and she
Is lovelier far, O Queen! than thee."

Then the Queen was very alarmed; for she knew that the glass always spoke the truth, and was sure that the servant had betrayed her. And she could not bear to think that any one lived who was more beautiful than she was; so she disguised herself as an old pedlar, and went her way over the hills to the place where the dwarfs dwelt. Then she knocked at the door, and cried, "Fine wares to sell!" Snow-drop looked out at the window and said, "Good-day, good woman; what have you to sell?" "Good wares, fine wares," said she; "laces and bobbins of all colours." "I will let the old lady in; she seems to be a very good sort of body," thought Snow-drop; so she ran down, and unbolted the door. "Bless me!" said the old woman, "how badly your stays are laced! Let me lace them up with one of my nice new laces." Snow-drop did not dream of any mischief; so she stood up before the old woman; but she set to work so nimbly, and pulled the lace so tight, that

Snow-drop lost her breath, and fell down as if she were dead. "There's an end of all thy beauty," said the spiteful Queen, and went away home.

In the evening the seven dwarfs returned; and I need not say how grieved they were to see their faithful Snow-drop stretched upon the ground motionless, as if she were quite dead. However, they lifted her up, and when they found what was the matter, they cut the lace; and in a little time she began to breathe, and soon came to life again. Then they said, "The old woman was the Queen herself; take care another time, and let no one in when we are away."

When the Queen got home, she went straight to her glass, and spoke to it as usual; but to her great surprise it still said:

"Thou, Queen, art the fairest in all this land;
But over the hills, in the greenwood shade,
Where the seven dwarfs their dwelling have made,
There Snow-drop is hiding her head; and she
Is lovelier far, O Queen! than thee."

Then the blood ran cold in her heart with spite and malice to see that Snow-drop still lived; and she dressed herself up again in a disguise, but very different from the one she wore before, and took with her a poisoned comb. When she reached the dwarfs' cottage, she knocked at the door, and cried, "Fine wares to sell;" but Snow-drop said, "I dare not let any one in." Then the Queen said, "Only look at my beautiful combs;" and gave her the poisoned one. And it looked so pretty that she took it up and put it into her hair to try it; but the moment it touched her head the poison was so powerful that she fell down senseless. "There you may lie," said the Queen, and went her way. But by good luck the dwarfs returned very early that evening; and when they saw Snow-drop lying on the ground, they thought what had happened, and soon found the poisoned comb. And when they took it away, she recovered, and told them all that had passed; and they warned her once more not to open the door to anyone.

Meantime the Queen went home to her glass, and trembled with rage when she received exactly the same

answer as before; and she said, "Snow-drop shall die, if it costs me my life." So she went secretly into a chamber, and prepared a poisoned apple: the outside looked very rosy and tempting, but whoever tasted it was sure to die. Then she dressed herself up as a peasant's wife, and travelled over the hills to the dwarfs' cottage, and knocked at the door; but Snow-drop put her head out of the window, and said, "I dare not let anyone in, for the dwarfs have told me not." "Do as you please," said the old woman, "but at any rate take this pretty apple; I will make you a present of it." "No," said Snow-drop, "I dare not take it." "You silly girl!" answered the other, "what are you afraid of? do you think it is poisoned? Come! do you eat one part, and I will eat the other." Now the apple was so prepared that one side was good, though the other side was poisoned. Then Snow-drop was very much tempted to taste, for the apple looked exceedingly nice; and when she saw the old woman eat, she could refrain no longer. But she had scarcely put the piece into her mouth when she fell down dead upon the ground. "This time nothing will save thee," said the Queen; and she went home to her glass, and at last it said:

"Thou, Queen, art the fairest of all the fair."

And then her envious heart was glad, and as happy as such a heart could be.

When evening came, and the dwarfs returned home, they found Snow-drop lying on the ground: no breath passed her lips, and they were afraid that she was quite dead. They lifted her up, and combed her hair, and washed her face with wine and water; but all was in vain, for the little girl seemed quite dead. So they laid her down upon a bier, and all seven watched and bewailed her three

whole days; and then they proposed to bury her; but her cheeks were still rosy, and her face looked just as it did while she was alive; so they said, "We will never bury her in the cold ground." And they made a coffin of glass so that they might still look at her, and wrote her name upon it, in golden letters, and that she was a king's daughter. And the coffin was placed upon the hill, and one of the dwarfs always sat by it, and watched. And the birds of the air came too, and bemoaned Snow-drop; first of all came an owl, and then a raven, but at last came a dove.

And thus Snow-drop lay for a long long time, and still only looked as though she was asleep; for she was even now as white as snow, and as red as blood, and as black as ebony. At last a Prince came and called at the dwarfs' house; and he saw Snow-drop, and read what was written in golden letters. Then he offered the dwarfs money, and earnestly prayed them to let him take her away; but they said, "We will not part with her for all the gold in the world." At last, however, they had pity on him, and gave him the coffin; but the moment he lifted it up to carry it home with him, the piece of apple fell from between her lips, and Snow-drop awoke, and said, "Where am I?" And the Prince answered, "Thou art safe with me." Then he told her all that had happened, and said, "I love you better than all the world; come with me to my father's palace, and you will be my wife." And Snow-drop consented, and went home with the Prince; and everything was prepared with great pomp and splendour for their wedding.

To the feast was invited, among the rest, Snow-drop's old enemy, the Queen; and as she was dressing herself in fine rich clothes, she looked in the glass and said:

"Tell me, glass, tell me true!
Of all the ladies in the land,
Who is fairest? tell me who?"

And the glass answered:

"Thou, lady, art loveliest here, I ween;
But lovelier far is the new-made Queen."

When she heard this, she started with rage; but her envy and curiosity were so great, that she could not help setting out to see the bride. And when she arrived, and saw that it was no other than Snow-drop, who, as she thought, had been dead a long while, she choked with passion, and fell ill and died; but Snow-drop and the Prince lived and reigned happily over that land many many years.

Pavane for Marie Antoinette

In Four Movements

i

A Poet describes her

"The queen of curds and cream."

Such was Will Shakespeare's description of Perdita, the dairymaid princess in *A Winter's Tale*.

Such might have been his description of Marie Antoinette, the light-hearted Queen of France, who lost her head in the French Revolution. But until the Revolution broke out in 1789 she played with her courtiers at being shepherds and shepherdesses in the Petit Trianon, her make-believe farm in the palace gardens of Versailles; where (still in the Poet's words) she danced like "a wave o' the sea".

ii

A Politician adores her

Mr. Edmund Burke writes:

"It is now sixteen or seventeen years since I saw the Queen of France, then the Dauphiness, at Versailles; and surely never lighted on this orb, which she hardly seemed to touch, a more delightful vision. I saw her just above the horizon, decorating and cheering the elevated sphere she just began to move in—glittering like the morning star, full of life, and splendour, and joy. . . . Little did I dream that I should have lived to see disasters fallen upon her in a nation of gallant men, in a nation of men of honour, and of cavaliers. I thought ten thousand swords must have leaped from their scabbards to avenge even a look that threatened her with insult. But the age of chivalry is gone. That of sophisters, economists, and calculators, has succeeded; and the glory of Europe is extinguished for ever."

From *Reflections on the Revolution in France*

iii

Her Epitaph

On the Toilet Table of
Queen Marie-Antoinette

This was her table, these her trim outspread
Brushes and trays and porcelain cups for red;
Here sate she, while her women tired and curled
The most unhappy head in all the world.

J. B. B. Nichols

iv

Her Monument

Baked by a Queen of the Kitchen

"Qu'ils mangent les brioches!" "Let them eat cake!" said this light-hearted, light-footed, light-minded Queen, when she heard that the poor citizens of Paris had no bread.

From Mrs. Beeton's Cookery Book

QUEEN CAKES

INGREDIENTS—1 lb of flour, ½ lb of butter, ½ lb of castor sugar, 3 eggs, 1 teacupful of baking-powder, essence of lemon or almonds, to taste.

METHOD—Sieve the baking-powder well with the flour on to a sheet of paper. Put the butter, sugar, and cream into a clean basin, and beat up to a light cream. Add the eggs one at a time. When all the eggs are in, add the flour and fruit, and moisten with milk to the consistency of cake-batter. Put it into small buttered tins, and bake the cakes from ¼ to ½ an hour. Grated lemond-rind may be substituted for the lemon and almond flavouring, and will make the cakes equally nice.

TIME—¼ to ½ an hour.

AVERAGE COST—1s. 9d.

Sufficient for two or three dozen small cakes.

Royal Blue

WILLIAM MAYNE

Those are the names of this story and its author. A year ago, in The Book of Kings, *I tried to tell you what William Mayne is like. Nobody tries that twice, so this year I'll try to tell you what he isn't like. It may be of some help. If you looked for him in the Aviary at the Zoo, he would be more like a Canary than a Cockatoo. If you looked for him in a wood, he would be more like a Spindle-tree than a Scotch Fir. If you planted him in your garden, he would come up more like Mignonette than Red Hot Pokers. If you framed him and hung him on your wall, he would look more like a Lake painted by Monet than a Storm at Sea by Turner. If you ordered him for lunch at a quiet but exclusive restaurant, he would taste more like Dover Sole with Muscatels than Indian Curry with Poppadums.* If you painted your front door green with him, it would be more* Eau-de-nil *than Emerald. If you played him in the Festival Hall, he would sound more like a Haydn Trio than a Liszt Rhapsody. And if you played him on Lord's Cricket-Ground, he would be more like a Leg-Glance than a Drive through the Covers for Six. That's all I can say about what William Mayne isn't. Make whatever else you can of him. I can't.*

E.F.

**P.S. On second thoughts, he might conceivably be not utterly unlike* one *Poppadum.*

E.F.

SOMETIMES there was a sentry in the box outside the Palace. Usually the box was empty. At other times a black and white island dog would sleep there. Today there was no sentry, and no dog. Tevita thought he might be able to go down by the garden wall of the Palace and climb the pine tree by the edge of the sea. The tree wasn't in the Palace garden, but on the malai, the green lawn that belonged to the town. The tree didn't belong to the Queen, or to her grandchildren. Tevita had seen the grandchildren climbing it. They were bigger than he was, but he thought he could climb just as well.

A pine tree is different from a coconut tree. Coconut trees are not hard to climb: you just hold on for a long time, all the way up and all the way down, with a knife stuck in your belt. Then at the top you hold on to a leaf and take the knife out, cut off a nut or two, and hurry down the tree before your friends take the nuts for themselves. Climbing for nuts is like climbing a thick rope. Climbing a pine tree is like climbing a thick wall, very rough, until you get among the branches. Tevita thought he would go round to the far side of the tree, out of sight of the Palace, out of sight of the town, and climb there, on the seaward side.

There was no one about. Tevita ran down beside the white wall to the corner. The sea was licking the sand quietly, and the tide was up. A hundred yards out to sea the Pacific was beating against the reef, just as if the island were being driven into the deep water like a steamship. Inside the reef the water was calm and the waves little.

Tevita took a run at the tree, clinging to the bark with fingers and toes. As he went up the run changed to a walk, and from a walk to a standstill. His feet came closer to his hands. He stood out from the side of the tree like a caterpillar. Then he fell off.

He looked at the tree, when he was on the ground, and thought he had been climbing the steepest part of it. When he stood up he moved round a little, and took a

few steps back to take another run. He walked backwards into one of the Queen's guns, a cannon that stood there to keep off enemy canoes in the days when there were enemies to fight. There were no enemies now.

This time he got further up the tree. He came to a standstill again, but he did not let his feet go on walking until he lost his balance with it. He clung on whilst he was comfortable, and looked upwards to see where to go next.

The first branch was just above him. He held on with his toes and reached up with one hand. His fingers just touched the branch. He stretched up still more, and thought he might be able to jump up the rest of the way and get an arm round the branch. He was in the middle of getting ready for the jump when somebody spoke to him.

At first he thought the voice was in the tree. It said, "Boy." He looked up, and there was no one above him. He looked down, and there was someone standing below, on the ground. It was a very tall lady, and she was looking up at him. Tevita stopped climbing. He stopped holding. He tried to turn round, because it was disrespectful to turn your back on the Queen. He did turn round, but he could not hold on at the same time, so he fell out of the tree again. It was uncomfortable, because he was sliding down the trunk, and it was scraping his back and pulling his shirt out from his pants. For a moment he could not think of anything worse in the world than being in front of the Queen with no shirt on.

He stopped sliding. The Queen had put out a hand and caught him. His feet touched the ground, and he stood up. At least he had not rolled about on the ground with his shirt out. He put his hand behind him and tucked the shirt in. The Queen let go of him.

"What is your name?" she said, in English.

Tevita knew English. He knew just that much English, at any rate, because he had learnt it at school. He answered in English.

"My name is Tevita, Your Majesty."

"Your name is David," said the Queen. Tevita knew that was right, because David was the English for Tevita.

"My name is David," he said.

"David," said the Queen, "go to the store and buy me a bottle of ink." This time she spoke in his own language, and he knew what it meant. He thought she might talk in English all the time, because she knew English perfectly well.

"Ink," said Tevita.

"Bring it back to me in the Palace garden," said the Queen. "I shall be sitting there. I was writing a letter, but the ink bottle is dry."

"I have not learnt writing," said Tevita.

The Queen smiled. She gave Tevita a shilling. "You will keep the change," she said.

Tevita ran across the malai feeling very rich. It was not his own shilling, but he would be able to spend some of it for himself. Now it was still a shilling belonging to the Queen. It had the Queen of England's head on it, though.

He came to the cross-roads in the middle of the town. There was a policeman in the box in the middle of the roads, directing the traffic. Tevita waited until a lorry had stopped. Then he ran across the road in front of it, and up the steps into the store, among all the counters. The clerk at the first counter wanted to send him away, but he waved the shilling in his face. The clerk went back to his place. He thinks I am rich, said Tevita to himself.

"Ink," he said. "Where is the ink?"

The clerk pointed across the store to another counter.

Tevita ran round two corners and came to the place. He was not tall enough to see over the counter, so he went round to the end of it, and looked along behind.

"Ink," he said. "I want a bottle of ink."

"What colour?" said the girl.

"Oh," said Tevita. "She did not say what colour."

"What colour did you have last time?" said the girl.

"We have never had any ink in our house," said Tevita. "It is for the Queen. She sent me."

"Royal Blue," said the girl. "We have sent it to the Palace plenty of times." She put her hand up to the shelf and brought out a little box."

"It is a bottle I was sent for," said Tevita.

The girl opened the box. "There is a bottle inside," she said. "Look."

Tevita looked, and saw. There was a bottle inside.

"That is right," he said. "She is writing a letter to the Queen of England."

"Of course," said the girl. "She only writes to Queens."

She gave the ink to Tevita, and went to attend to another customer. On the way to the other customer she wrote in a book. She did not take Tevita's shilling.

"Wait," he said. "Where is the change?"

The girl came back to him. "We will send a bill to the Palace," she said. "It is the usual thing to do. The Queen will give you a penny for running the errand. Queens do."

Tevita put the shilling, quite unused, and the new ink into one hand together, and started to go out of the store. Then he thought that he wasn't doing what the Queen had told him to do. A whole shilling was not change. It was just money not spent. But the Queen would not give him a whole shilling. No one would. He went back to the counter, and to the end of it again.

"I have served you," said the girl.

"Here is my shilling," said Tevita. "Take the money from it for the ink, and give me the change, because that is what the Queen said."

The girl took the shilling. She wrote in her book again. "That is all," she said.

"You must give me my change," said Tevita.

"There is no change," said the girl. "The price of ink is a shilling. Whatever I do, there will be no change. If I write it down there will be that shilling to take back. If I do not write it down there will be nothing to take back."

Tevita looked at the girl. "You are very stupid," he said. "You must charge less for the ink. The Queen wants some change. She will write about you to the Queen of England."

"There is no change," said the girl.

Then there was a hand on Tevita's shoulder. It belonged to the manager of the store. "What are you making a fuss about?" he said.

The girl began to tell him. When she had finished the manager thought for a moment. "This is what we will do," he said. "We will write down the bill, and we will take the shilling, but we will give this boy . . ."

"Tevita," said Tevita.

"Tevita," said the manager. "We will give him the shilling all in little money, all in change. The Queen will be pleased to have all her money in change." Then he took the shilling from Tevita, put it in his own pocket, and gave Tevita a handful of other coins. "Run along," he said.

Tevita ran along. He crossed the road again, with the ink in one hand and the money in the other, and ran across the malai, to the sentry box by the Palace gate.

There he stopped, put the money and the ink on the ground, and made sure his shirt was tucked in straight. He picked up the ink and the money, and walked through the gate.

The Queen was sitting in the garden. In front of her was a little table, with papers on it, and a pen lying on top of the papers. There was an ink bottle there too, but it had no box round it.

"David," said the Queen. "Take the ink out of the box. Now take the top off the bottle, and put the bottle on the table."

Tevita had to put the money down on the grass so that he could use both hands.

"This is too much money," the Queen said.

She leaned over and touched the money. Tevita was going to try to explain why there was so much, but he did not know where to begin.

"Do not make faces," said the Queen, when she had looked at the money. "They have written it down at the store, I think."

"The shilling is all changed," said Tevita. "It is what you said."

"It is more than I said," said the Queen. "Pick up a Trey. Now take it and spend it. You are a good boy."

Tevita picked up a threepenny piece when he had put the ink bottle on the table. Then he thought for a moment, and spoke in English. "Thank you, Your Majesty," he said.

"Thank you, David," said the Queen, and dipped her pen in the new ink.

Henry VIII

Bluff King Hal was full of beans;
He married half a dozen queens;
For three called Kate they cried the banns,
And one called Jane, and a couple of Annes.

The first he asked to share his reign
Was Kate of Aragon, straight from Spain—
But when his love for her was spent,
He got a divorce, and out she went.

Anne Boleyn was his second wife;
He swore to cherish her all his life—
But seeing a third he wished instead,
He chopped off poor Anne Boleyn's head.

He married the next afternoon
Jane Seymour, which was rather soon—
But after one year as his bride
She crept into her bed and died.

Anne of Cleves was Number Four;
Her portrait thrilled him to the core—
But when he met her face to face
Another royal divorce took place.

Catherine Howard, Number Five,
Billed and cooed to keep alive—
But one day Henry felt depressed;
The executioner did the rest.

Sixth and last came Catherine Parr,
Sixth and last and luckiest far—
For this time it was Henry who
Hopped the twig, and a good job too.

Eleanor and Herbert Farjeon
Kings and Queens

Gloriana

RUDYARD KIPLING

Gloriana *was England's famous Queen, Elizabeth, who never married anyone. She would have been a lively wife if she had, I think. She kept arranging to get married, mostly to enemies, because whilst she was considering a foreign king he couldn't very well start a war against England—it would have been unfriendly. But Elizabeth was more concerned with England than with husbands. She was a great Queen, but it was a pity she had to lop off the head of her Stuart cousin, Mary, Queen of Scotland. Another Stuart who had his head cut off, later on, was actually King of England when it was done—you weren't safe anywhere in those days.*

The story here comes from those written by Rudyard Kipling in the books, Puck of Pook's Hill *and* Rewards and Fairies. *Puck is a tricksy but friendly goblin who appears from time to time to Dan and Una, and brings them back into History, where they meet people and hear stories.*

W.M.

WILLOW SHAW, the little fenced wood where the hop-poles are stacked like Indian wigwams, had been given to Dan and Una for their very own kingdom when they were quite small. As they grew older, they contrived to keep it most particularly private. Even Phillips, the gardener, told them every time he came in to take a hop-pole for his beans, and old Hobden would no more have thought of setting his rabbit-wires there without leave, given fresh each spring, than he would have torn down the calico and marking-ink notice on the big willow which said: "Grown-ups not allowed in the Kingdom unless brought."

Now you can understand their indignation when, one blowy July afternoon, as they were going up for a potato-roast, they saw somebody moving among the trees. They hurled themselves over the gate, dropping half the potatoes, and while they were picking them up Puck came out of a wigwam.

"Oh, it's you, is it?" said Una. "We thought it was people."

"I saw you were angry—from your legs," he answered with a grin.

"Well, it's our own Kingdom—not counting you, of course."

"That's rather why I came. A lady here wants to see you."

"What about?" said Dan cautiously.

"Oh, just Kingdoms and things. She knows about Kingdoms."

There was a lady near the fence dressed in a long dark cloak that hid everything except her high red-heeled shoes. Her face was half covered by a black silk fringed mask, without goggles. And yet she did not look in the least as if she motored.

Puck led them up to her and bowed solemnly. Una made the best dancing-lesson curtsy she could remember. The lady answered with a long, deep, slow, billowy one.

"Since it seems that you are a Queen of this Kingdom," she said, "I can do no less than acknowledge your sovereignty." She turned sharply on staring Dan. "What's in your head, lad? Manners?"

"I was thinking how wonderfully you did that curtsy," he answered.

She laughed a rather shrill laugh. "You're a courtier

already. Do you know anything of dances, wench—or Queen, must I say?"

"I've had some lessons, but I can't really dance a bit," said Una.

"You should learn then." The lady moved forward as though she would teach her at once. "It gives a woman alone among men or her enemies time to think how she shall win or—lose. A woman can only work in man's play-time. Heigho!" She sat down on the bank.

Old Middenboro, the lawn-mower pony, stumped across the paddock and hung his sorrowful head over the fence.

"A pleasant Kingdom," said the lady, looking round. "Well enclosed. And how does your Majesty govern it? Who is your Minister?"

Una did not quite understand. "We don't play that," she said.

"Play?" The lady threw up her hands and laughed.

"We have it for our own, together," Dan explained.

"And d'you never quarrel, young Burleigh?"

"Sometimes, but then we don't tell."

The lady nodded. "I've no brats of my own but I understand keeping a secret between Queens and their Ministers. Ay de mi! But with no disrespect to present majesty, methinks your realm is small, and therefore likely to be coveted by man and beast. For example"—she pointed to Middenboro—"yonder old horse, with the face of a Spanish friar—does he never break in?"

"He can't. Old Hobden stops all our gaps for us," said Una, "and we let Hobden catch rabbits in the Shaw."

The lady laughed like a man. "I see! Hobden catches conies—rabbits—for himself, and guards your defences for you. Does he make a profit out of his coney-catching?"

"We never ask," said Una. "Hobden's a particular friend of ours."

"Hoity-toity!" the lady began angrily. Then she laughed. "But I forget. It is your Kingdom. I knew a maid once that had a larger one than this to defend, and so long as her men kept the fences stopped, she asked 'em no questions either."

"Was she trying to grow flowers?" said Una.

"No, trees—perdurable trees. Her flowers all withered." The lady leaned her head on her hand.

"They do if you don't look after them. We've got a few. Would you like to see? I'll fetch you some." Una ran off to the rank grass in the shade behind the wigwam, and came back with a handful of red flowers. "Aren't they pretty?" she said. "They're Virginia stock."

"Virginia?" said the lady, and lifted them to the fringe of her mask.

"Yes. They come from Virginia. Did your maid ever plant any?"

"Not herself—but her men adventured all over the earth to pluck or to plant flowers for her crown. They judged her worthy of them."

"And was she?" said Dan cheerfully.

"Quien sabe? (who knows?) But at least, while her men toiled abroad she toiled in England, that they might find a safe home to come back to."

"And what was she called?"

"Gloriana—Belphoebe—Elizabeth of England." Her voice changed at each word.

"You mean Queen Bess?" The lady bowed her head a little towards Dan.

"You name her lightly enough, young Burleigh. What might you know of her?" said she.

"Well, I—I've seen the little green shoes she left at Brickwall House—down the road, you know. They're in a glass case—awfully tiny things."

"Oh, Burleigh, Burleigh!" she laughed. "You are a courtier too soon."

"But they are," Dan insisted. "As little as dolls' shoes. Did you really know her well?"

"Well. She was a woman. I've been at her Court all my life. Yes, I remember when she danced after the banquet at Brickwall. They say she danced Philip of Spain out of a brand-new kingdom that day. Worth the price of a pair of old shoes—hey?"

She thrust out one foot, and stooped forward to look at its broad flashing buckle.

"You've heard of Philip of Spain—long-suffering Philip?" she said, her eyes still on the shining stones. "Faith, what some men will endure at some women's hands passes belief! If I had been a man, and a woman had played with me as Elizabeth played with Philip, I would have—" she nipped off one of the Virginia stocks and held it up between finger and thumb. "But for all that"—she began to strip the leaves one by one—"they say—and I am persuaded—that Philip loved her." She tossed her head sideways.

"I don't quite understand," said Una.

"The high heavens forbid that you should, wench!" She swept the flowers from her lap and stood up in the rush of shadows that the wind chased through the wood.

"I should like to know about the shoes," said Dan.

"So ye shall, Burleigh. So ye shall, if ye watch me. 'Twill be as good as a play."

"We've never been to a play," said Una.

The lady looked at her and laughed. "I'll make one for

you. Watch! You are to imagine that she—Gloriana, Belphoebe, Elizabeth—has gone on a progress to Rye to comfort her sad heart (maids are often melancholic), and while she halts at Brickwall House, the village—what was its name?" She pushed Puck with her foot.

"Norgem," he croaked, and squatted by the wigwam.

"Norgem village loyally entertains her with a masque or play, and a Latin oration spoken by the parson, for whose false quantities, if I'd made 'em in my girlhood, I should have been whipped."

"You whipped?" said Dan.

"Soundly, sirrah, soundly! She stomachs the affront to her scholarship, makes her grateful, gracious thanks from the teeth outwards, thus"—(the lady yawned)—"Oh, a Queen may love her subjects in her heart, and yet be dog-wearied of 'em in body and mind—and so sits down"—her skirts foamed about her as she sat—"to a banquet beneath Brickwall Oak. Here for her sins she is waited upon by—What were the young cockerels' names that served Gloriana at table?"

"Frewens, Courthopes, Fullers, Husseys," Puck began.

She held up her long jewelled hand. "Spare the rest! They were the best blood of Sussex, and by so much the more clumsy in handling the dishes and plates. Wherefore"—she looked funnily over her shoulder—"you are to think of Gloriana in a green and gold-laced habit, dreadfully expecting that the jostling youths behind her would, of pure jealousy or devotion, spatter it with sauces and wines. The gown was Philip's gift, too! At this happy juncture a Queen's messenger, mounted and mired, spurs up the Rye road and delivers her a letter"—she giggled—"a letter from a good, simple, frantic Spanish gentleman called—Don Philip."

"That wasn't Philip, King of Spain?" Dan asked.

"Truly, it was 'Twixt you and me and the bedpost, young Burleigh, these kings and queens are very like men and women, and I've heard they write each other fond, foolish letters that none of their ministers should open."

"Did her ministers ever open Queen Elizabeth's letters?" said Una.

"Faith, yes! But she'd have done as much for theirs, any day. You are to think of Gloriana, then (they say she had a pretty hand), excusing herself thus to the company—for the Queen's time is never her own—and, while the music strikes up, reading Philip's letter, as I do." She drew a real letter from her pocket, and held it out almost at arm's length, like the old post-mistress in the village when she reads telegrams.

"Hm! Hm! Hm! Philip writes as ever most lovingly. He says his Gloriana is cold, for which reason he burns for her through a fair written page." She turned it with a snap. "What's here? Philip complains that certain of her gentlemen have fought against his generals in the Low Countries. He prays her to hang 'em when they re-enter her realms. (Hm, that's as may be.) Here's a list of burnt shipping slipped between two vows of burning adoration. Oh, poor Philip! His admirals at sea—no less than three of 'em—have been boarded, sacked, and scuttled on their lawful voyages by certain English mariners (gentlemen, he will not call them), who are now at large and working more piracies in his American ocean, which the Pope gave him. (He and the Pope should guard it, then!) Philip hears, but his devout ears will not credit it, that Gloriana in some fashion countenances these villains' misdeeds, shares in their booty, and—oh, shame!—has even lent them ships royal for their sinful thefts. Therefore he

requires (which is a word Gloriana loves not), *requires* that she shall hang 'em when they return to England, and afterwards shall account to him for all the goods and gold they have plundered. A most loving request! If Gloriana will not be Philip's bride, she shall be his broker and his butcher! Should she still be stiff-necked, he writes—see where the pen digged the innocent paper!—that he hath both the means and the intention to be revenged on her. Aha! Now we come to the Spaniard in his shirt!" (She waved the letter merrily.) "Listen here! Philip will prepare for Gloriana a destruction from the West—a destruction from the West—far exceeding that which Pedro de Avila wrought upon the Huguenots. And he rests and remains, kissing her feet and her hands, her slave, her enemy, or her conqueror, as he shall find that she uses him."

She thrust back the letter under her cloak, and went on acting, but in a softer voice. "All this while—hark to it—the wind blows through Brickwall Oak, the music plays, and, with the company's eyes upon her, the Queen of England must think what this means. She cannot remember the name of Pedro de Avila, nor what he did to the Huguenots, nor when, nor where. She can only see darkly some dark motion moving in Philip's dark mind, for he hath never written before in this fashion. She must smile above the letter as though it were good news from her ministers—the smile that tires the mouth and the poor heart. What shall she do?" Again her voice changed.

"You are to fancy that the music of a sudden wavers away. Chris Hatton, Captain of her bodyguard, quits the table all red and ruffled, and Gloriana's virgin ear catches the clash of swords at work behind a wall. The mothers of Sussex look round to count their chicks—I mean those young game-cocks that waited on her. Two dainty youths have stepped aside into Brickwall garden with rapier and dagger on a private point of honour. They are haled out through the gate, disarmed and glaring—the lively image of a brace of young Cupids transformed into pale panting Cains. Ahem! Gloriana beckons awfully—thus! They come up for judgment. Their lives and estates lie at her mercy whom they have doubly offended, both as Queen and woman. But la! what will not foolish young men do for a beautiful maid?"

"Why? What did she do? What had they done?" said Una.

"Hsh! You mar the play! Gloriana had guessed the cause of the trouble. They were handsome lads. So she frowns a while and tells 'em not to be bigger fools than their mothers had made 'em, and warns 'em, if they do not kiss and be friends on the instant, she'll have Chris Hatton horse and birch 'em in the style of the new school at Harrow. (Chris looks sour at that.) Lastly, because she needed time to think on Philip's letter burning in her pocket, she signifies her pleasure to dance with 'em and teach 'em better manners. Whereat the revived company call down Heaven's blessing on her gracious head; Chris and the others prepare Brickwall House for a dance, and she walks in the clipped garden between those two lovely young sinners who are both ready to sink for shame. They confess their fault. It appears that midway in the banquet the elder—they were cousins—conceived that the Queen looked upon him with special favour. The younger, taking the look to himself, after some words gives the elder the lie; hence, as she guessed, the duel."

"And which had she really looked at?" Dan asked.

"Neither—except to wish them farther off. She was afraid all the while they'd spill dishes on her gown. She tells 'em this, poor chicks—and it completes their abasement. When they had grilled long enough, she says: 'And so you would have fleshed your maiden swords for me—for me?' Faith, they would have been at it again if she'd egged 'em on! but their swords—oh, prettily, they said it! —had been drawn for her once or twice already.

" 'And where?' says she. 'On your hobby-horses before you were breeched?'

" 'On my own ship,' says the elder. 'My cousin was vice-admiral of our venture in his pinnace. We would not have you think of us as brawling children.'

" 'No, no,' says the younger, and flames like a very Tudor rose. 'At least the Spaniards know us better.'

" 'Admiral Boy—Vice-Admiral Babe,' says Gloriana, 'I cry your pardon. The heat of these present times ripens childhood to age more quickly than I can follow. But we are at peace with Spain. Where did you break your Queen's peace?'

" 'On the sea called the Spanish Main, though 'tis no more Spanish than my doublet,' says the elder. Guess how that warmed Gloriana's already melting heart! She would never suffer any sea to be called Spanish in her private hearing.

" 'And why was I not told? What booty got you, and where have you hid it? Disclose,' says she. 'You stand in some danger of the gallows for pirates.'

" 'The axe, most gracious lady,' says the elder, 'for we are gentle born.' He spoke truth, but no woman can brook contradiction. 'Hoity-toity,' says she, and, but that she remembered that she was a Queen, she'd have cuffed the pair of 'em. 'It shall be gallows, hurdle, and dung-cart if I choose.'

" 'Had our Queen known of our going beforehand, Philip might have held her to blame for some small things we did on the seas,' the younger lisps.

" 'As for treasure,' says the elder, 'we brought back but our bare lives. We were wrecked on the Gascons' Graveyard, where our sole company for three months was the bleached bones of De Avila's men.'

"Gloriana's mind jumped back to Philip's last letter.

" 'De Avila that destroyed the Huguenots? What d'you know of him?' she says. The music called from the house here, and they three turned back between the yews.

" 'Simply that De Avila broke in upon a plantation of Frenchmen on that coast, and very Spaniardly hung them all for heretics—eight hundred or so. The next year Dominique de Gorgues, a Gascon, broke in upon De Avila's men, and very justly hung 'em all for murderers—five hundred or so. No Christians inhabit there now,' says the elder lad, 'though 'tis a goodly land north of Florida.'

" 'How far is it from England?' asks prudent Gloriana.

" 'With a fair wind, six weeks. They say that Philip will plant it again soon.' This was the younger, and he looked at her out of the corner of his innocent eye.

"Chris Hatton, fuming, meets and leads her into Brick-wall Hall, where she dances—thus. A woman can think while she dances—can think. I'll show you. Watch!"

She took off her cloak slowly, and stood forth in dove-coloured satin, worked over with pearls that trembled like running water in the running shadows of the trees. Still talking—more to herself than to the children—she swam into a majestical dance of the stateliest balancings, the haughtiest wheelings and turnings aside, the most dignified sinkings, the gravest risings, all joined together by the elaboratest interlacing steps and circles.

They leaned forward breathlessly to watch the splendid acting.

"Would a Spaniard," she began, looking on the ground, "speak of his revenge till his revenge were ripe? No. Yet a man who loved a woman might threaten her in the hope that his threats would make her love him. Such things have been." She moved slowly across a bar of sunlight. "A destruction from the West may signify that Philip means to descend on Ireland. But then my Irish spies would have had some warning. The Irish keep no secrets. No—'tis not Ireland. Now why—why—why"—the red shoes clicked and paused—"does Philip name Pedro Melendez de Avila, a general in his Americas, unless"—she turned more quickly—"unless he intends to work his destruction from the Americas? Did he say De Avila only to put her off her guard, or for this once has his black pen betrayed his black heart? We"—she raised herself to her full height—"England must forestall Master Philip. But not openly," she sank again—"we cannot fight Spain openly—not yet—not yet." She stepped three paces as though she were pegging down some snare with her twinkling shoe-buckles. "The Queen's mad gentlemen may fight Philip's poor admirals where they find 'em, but England, Gloriana, Harry's daughter, must keep the peace. Perhaps, after all, Philip loves her—as many men and boys do. That may help England. Oh, *what* shall help England?"

She raised her head—the masked head that seemed to have nothing to do with the busy feet—and stared straight at the children.

"I think this is rather creepy," said Una with a shiver. "I wish she'd stop."

The lady held out her jewelled hand as though she were taking someone else's hand in the Grand Chain.

"Can a ship go down into the Gascons' Graveyard and wait there?" she asked into the air, and passed on rustling.

"She's pretending to ask one of the cousins, isn't she?" said Dan, and Puck nodded.

Back she came in the silent, swaying, ghostly dance. They saw she was smiling beneath the mask, and they could hear her breathing hard.

"I cannot lend you any of my ships for the venture; Philip would hear of it," she whispered over her shoulder; "but as much guns and powder as you ask, if you do not ask too—" her voice shot up and she stamped her foot thrice. "Louder! Louder, the music in the gallery! Oh, me, but I have burst out of my shoe!"

She gathered her skirts in each hand, and began a curtsy. "You will go at your own charges," she whispered straight before her. "Oh, enviable and adorable age of youth!" Her eyes shone through the mask-holes. "But I warn you you'll repent it. Put not your trust in princes—or Queens. Philip's ships'll blow you out of water. You'll not be frightened? Well, we'll talk on it again, when I return from Rye, dear lads."

The wonderful curtsy ended. She stood up. Nothing stirred on her except the rush of the shadows.

"And so it was finished," she said to the children. "Why d'you not applaud?"

"What was finished?" said Una.

"The dance," the lady replied offendedly. "And a pair of green shoes."

"I don't understand a bit," said Una.

"Eh? What did *you* make of it, young Burleigh?"

"I'm not quite sure," Dan began, "but—"

"You never can be—with a woman. But—"

"But I thought Gloriana meant the cousins to go back to the Gascons' Graveyard, wherever that was."

"'Twas Virginia afterwards. Her plantation of Virginia."

"Virginia afterwards, and stop Philip from taking it. Didn't she say she'd lend 'em guns?"

"Right so. But not ships—*then*."

"And I thought you meant they must have told her

they'd do it off their own bat, without getting her into a row with Philip. Was I right?"

"Near enough for a Minister of the Queen. But remember she gave the lads full time to change their minds. She was three long days at Rye Royal—knighting of fat Mayors. When she came back to Brickwall, they met her a mile down the road, and she could feel their eyes burn through her riding-mask. Chris Hatton, poor fool, was vexed at it.

" 'You would not birch them when I gave you the chance,' says she to Chris. 'Now you must get me half an hour's private speech with 'em in Brickwall garden. Eve tempted Adam in a garden. Quick, man, or I may repent!' "

"She was a Queen. Why did she not send for them herself," said Una.

The lady shook her head. "That was never her way. I've seen her walk to her own mirror by bye-ends, and the woman that cannot walk straight *there* is past praying for. Yet I would have you pray for her! What else—what else in England's name could she have done?" She lifted her hand to her throat for a moment. "Faith," she cried, "I'd forgotten the little green shoes! She left 'em at Brickwall—so she did. And I remember she gave the Norgem parson—John Withers, was he?—a text for his sermon—'Over Edom have I cast out my shoe.' Neat, if he'd understood!"

"I don't understand," said Una. "What about the two cousins?"

"You are as cruel as a woman," the lady answered. "I was not to blame. I told you I gave 'em time to change their minds. On my honour (ay de mi!), she asked no more of 'em at first than to wait a while off that coast—the

Gascons' Graveyard—to hover a little if their ships chanced to pass that way—they had only one tall ship and a pinnace—only to watch and bring me word of Philip's doings. One must watch Philip always. What a murrain right had he to make any plantation there, a hundred leagues north of his Spanish Main, and only six weeks from England? By my dread father's soul, I tell you he had none—none!" She stamped her red foot again, and the two children shrunk back for a second.

"Nay, nay. You must not turn from me too! She laid it all fairly before the lads in Brickwall garden between the yews. I told 'em that if Philip sent a fleet (and to make a plantation he could not well send less), their poor little cock-boats could not sink it. They answered that, with submission, the fight would be their own concern. She showed 'em again that there could be only one end to it—quick death on the sea, or slow death in Philip's prisons. They asked no more than to embrace death for my sake. Many men have prayed to me for life. I've refused 'em, and slept none the worse after; but when my men, my tall, fantastical young men beseech me on their knees for leave to die for me, it shakes me—ah, it shakes me to the marrow of my old bones."

Her chest sounded like a board as she hit it.

"She showed 'em all. I told 'em that this was no time for open war with Spain. If by miracle inconceivable they prevailed against Philip's fleet, Philip would hold me accountable. For England's sake, to save war, I should e'en be forced (I told 'em so) to give him up their young lives. If they failed, and again by some miracle escaped Philip's hand, and crept back to England with their bare lives, they must lie—oh, I told 'em all—under my sovereign displeasure. She could not know them, see them, nor hear their names, nor stretch out a finger to save them from the gallows, if Philip chose to ask it.

" 'Be it the gallows, then,' says the elder. (I could have wept, but that my face was made for the day.)

" 'Either way—any way—this venture is death, which I know you fear not. But it is death with assured dishonour,' I cried.

" 'Yet our Queen will know in her heart what we have done,' says the younger.

" 'Sweetheart,' I said. 'A Queen has no heart.'

" 'But she is a woman, and a woman would not forget,' says the elder. 'We will go!' They knelt at my feet.

" 'Nay, dear lads—but here!' I said, and I opened my arms to them and I kissed them.

" 'Be ruled by me,' I said. 'We'll hire some ill-featured old tarry-breeks of an admiral to watch the Graveyard, and you shall come to Court.'

" 'Hire whom you please,' says the elder; 'we are ruled by you, body and soul'; and the younger, who shook most when I kissed 'em, says between his white lips, 'I think you have power to make a god of a man.'

" 'Come to Court and be sure of it,' I says.

"They shook their heads and I knew—I knew, that go they would. If I had not kissed them—perhaps I might have prevailed."

"Then why did you do it?" said Una. "I don't think you knew really what you wanted done."

"May it please your Majesty," the lady bowed her head low, "this Gloriana whom I have represented for your pleasure was a woman and a Queen. Remember her when you come to your kingdom."

"But did the cousins go to the Gascons' Graveyard?" said Dan, as Una frowned.

"They went," said the lady.

"Did they ever come back?" Una began; but—"Did they stop King Philip's fleet!" Dan interrupted.

The lady turned to him eagerly.

"D'you think they did right to go?" she asked.

"I don't see what else they could have done," Dan replied, after thinking it over.

"D'you think she did right to send 'em?" The lady's voice rose a little.

"Well," said Dan, "I don't see what else she could have done, either—do you? How did they stop King Philip from getting Virginia?"

"There's the sad part of it. They sailed out that autumn from Rye Royal, and there never came back so much as a single rope-yarn to show what had befallen them. The winds blew, and they were not. Does that make you alter your mind, young Burleigh?"

"I expect they were drowned, then. Anyhow, Philip didn't score, did he?"

"Gloriana wiped out her score with Philip later. But if Philip had won, would you have blamed Gloriana for wasting those lads' lives?'

"Of course not. She was bound to try to stop him."

The lady coughed. "You have the root of the matter in you. Were I Queen, I'd make you Minister."

"We don't play that game," said Una, who felt that she disliked the lady as much as she disliked the noise the high wind made tearing through Willow Shaw.

"Play!" said the lady with a laugh, and threw up her hands affectedly. The sunshine caught the jewels on her many rings and made them flash till Una's eyes dazzled, and she had to rub them. Then she saw Dan on his knees picking up the potatoes they had spilled at the gate.

"There wasn't anybody in the Shaw, after all," he said. "Didn't you think you saw someone?"

"I'm most awfully glad there isn't," said Una. Then they went on with the potato-roast.

Good Queen Bess

From *Queen Elizabeth I*

J. E. NEALE

FOR the remainder of his nine days' stay, Melville was in demand every day, and sometimes thrice in a day. He had spent many years in foreign courts and Elizabeth could therefore air her knowledge of French, Italian, and German—the last bad—and discuss the customs of other lands with him. Women's fashions being compared, each day she put on a different dress, one day English, another French, and a third Italian. She was delighted when Melville announced that the Italian style suited her best, as it showed her golden hair to advantage. She wanted to know what coloured hair was considered best, and how hers compared with Mary's. Then followed a whole series of comparisons. Who, she asked, was the fairer, Mary or she? a question Melville tried to dodge by declaring that she was the fairest Queen in England and theirs the fairest Queen in Scotland. As Elizabeth was not to be put off, he replied that they were both the fairest ladies of their courts, but the Queen of England was whiter, their Queen "very lusome". Next she wanted to know who was the higher. Mary was, answered Melville.

Then is she over high, retorted Elizabeth; she herself being neither over high nor over low. What, she asked, were Mary's amusements, and did she play well on the lute and the virginals? "Reasonably for a Queen," answered Melville. Here was a comparison that lent itself to demonstration. Accordingly that night the Queen's cousin, Lord Hunsdon, took Melville along to surprise Elizabeth, alone in her chamber, playing "exceedingly well" on the virginals. When she caught sight of him and chid him for being there without permission, he had his answer pat: "I heard such melody, which ravished and drew me within the chamber, I wist not how." His departure was delayed a night so that he could watch her dance and draw a final comparison. Mary, he announced, "danced not so high and disposedly as she did."

During his stay Melville had witnessed the creation of Dudley as Baron of Denbigh and Earl of Leicester, dignities which were meant to fit him to wed Mary. The ceremony was performed with great solemnity, but as the new earl knelt gravely before Elizabeth, her sense of fun got the better of her and she tickled his neck.

NOTE: Melville was sent to Queen Elizabeth's court from Mary Queen of Scots, to see about getting Mary married to Dudley; which is very strange, because Dudley was Elizabeth's favourite boy. In the end Elizabeth married no one, and Mary married several strange people.

QUEEN ELIZABETH AT TILBURY FORT

Riding on a war-charger, wearing armour, and holding a marshal's truncheon, she addresses her troops before the arrival of the Armada.

MY loving people, we have been persuaded by some

that are careful of our safety, to take heed how we commit ourselves to armed multitudes, for fear of treachery. But I assure you I do not desire to live to distrust my faithful and loving people. Let tyrants fear! I have always so behaved myself that, under God, I have placed my chiefest strength and safeguard in the loyal hearts and good-will of my subjects; and, not as for my recreation and sport, but being resolved in the midst and heat of the battle to live and die amongst you all—to lay down for my God, for my kingdom, and for my people, my honour and my blood, even in the dust. I know I have but the body of a weak and feeble woman; but I have the heart of a king, and of a King of England too, and think foul scorn that Parma, or Spain, or any prince of Europe, should dare to invade the borders of my realm! To which, rather than any dishonour shall grow by me, I myself will be your general, the judge and rewarder of every one of your virtues in the field. I know already by your forwardness, that you have deserved rewards and crowns; and we do assure you, on the word of a prince, they shall be duly paid you. In the meantime, my lieutenant-general shall be in my stead, than whom never prince commanded more noble or worthy subject. Nor will I suffer myself to doubt, but that by your obedience to my general, by the concord in the camp, and your valour in the field, we shall shortly have a famous victory over those enemies of my God, my kingdom, and my people.

From "Old and New London", Vol. IV, p. 118

THE first pair of silk stockings brought into England from Spain was presented to Henry VIII, who greatly prized them. In the third year of Elizabeth's reign, her "tiring" woman, Mrs Montagu, presented Her Majesty with a pair of black silk stockings as a new-year's present; whereupon Her Majesty asked if she could have any more, in which case she would wear no more cloth stockings.

From Chambers "Book of Days"

A WAGER is said to have been won by Sir Walter Raleigh from the Virgin Queen, on the question of how much smoke is obtained from a pound of tobacco. A pound of the article in question was weighed, burned, and then weighed again in ashes. The question was held to be satisfactorily settled by determining the weight of the smoke as exactly that of the tobacco, before being burned, minus the residuum of ashes. The fact of the ashes having received an additional weight by combination with the oxygen of the atmosphere, and also the circumstance of numerous imperceptible gases being evolved by the process of combustion, were alike unthought of by Elizabeth and her knight.

THERE SATE GOOD QUEEN BESS

WALTER DE LA MARE

There sate good Queen Bess, oh,
A-shining on her throne.
Up, Jessie; down docket;
My money's gone.

An Epigram addressed to Queen Caroline

the wife of George IV of England, who alas! was so unsatisfactory a Queen that a Royal Commission was appointed to investigate her conduct and her "carelessness of appearances".

Most Gracious Queen, we thee implore
To go away and sin no more,
But if that effort be too great,
To go away at any rate.

I suppose she was never brought up to brush her teeth and wash her face, but she apparently did try to be better, because later on they said:

Queen, Queen Caroline,
Washed her hair in turpentine;
Turpentine to make it shine,
Queen, Queen Caroline.

But don't you try it—shampoo does it better. But clean your teeth, or you'll never be Queen.

The Silly Jelly-Fish

A Japanese Story, told in English by
B. H. CHAMBERLAIN

ONCE upon a time the King of the Dragons, who had till then lived as a bachelor, took it into his head to get married. His bride was a young Dragonette just sixteen years old—lovely enough, in very sooth, to become the wife of a King. Great were the rejoicings on the occasion. The Fishes, both great and small, came to pay their respects, and to offer gifts to the newly wedded pair; and for some days all was feasting and merriment.

But alas! even Dragons have their trials. Before a month had passed, the young Dragon Queen fell ill. The doctors dosed her with every medicine that was known to them, but all to no purpose. At last they shook their heads, declaring that there was nothing more to be done. The illness must take its course, and she would probably die.

But the sick Queen said to her husband, "I know of something that would cure me. Only fetch me a live Monkey's liver to eat, and I shall get well at once."

"A live monkey's liver!" exclaimed the King. "What are you thinking of, my dear? Why! you forget that we Dragons live in the sea, while Monkeys live far away from here, among the forest-trees on land. A Monkey's liver! Why! darling, you must be mad."

Hereupon the young Dragon Queen burst into tears: "I only ask you for one small thing," whimpered she, "and you won't get it for me. I always thought you didn't really love me. Oh! I wish I had stayed at home with my own m-m-m-mama and my own papa-a-a-a!" Here her voice choked with sobs, and she could say no more.

Well, of course the Dragon King did not like to have it thought that he was unkind to his beautiful young wife. So he sent for his trusty servant the Jelly-Fish and said: "It is rather a difficult job; but what I want you to try to do is to swim across to the land, and persuade a live Monkey to come here with you. In order to make the Monkey willing to come, you can tell him how much nicer everything is here in Dragon-Land than away where he lives.

But what I really want him for is to cut out his liver, and use it as medicine for your young Mistress, who, as you know, is dangerously ill."

So the Jelly-Fish went off on his strange errand. In those days he was just like any other fish, with eyes, and fins, and a tail. He even had little feet, which made him able to walk on the land as well as to swim in the water. It did not take him many hours to swim across to the country where the Monkeys lived; and fortunately there just happened to be a fine Monkey skipping about among the branches of the trees near the place where the Jelly-Fish landed. So the Jelly-Fish said:

"Mr Monkey! I have come to tell you of a country far more beautiful than this. It lies beyond the waves, and is called Dragon-Land. There is pleasant weather there all the year round, there is always plenty of ripe fruit on the trees, and there are none of those mischievous creatures called Men. If you will come with me, I will take you there. Just get on my back."

The Monkey thought it would be fun to see a new country. So he leapt on to the Jelly-Fish's back, and off they started across the water. But when they had gone about half-way, he began to fear that perhaps there might be some hidden danger. It seemed so odd to be fetched suddenly in that way by a stranger. So he said to the Jelly-Fish: "What made you think of coming for me?"

The Jelly-Fish answered: "My Master, the King of the Dragons wants you in order to cut out your liver, and give it as medicine to his wife, the Queen who, is sick."

"Oh! that's your little game—is it?" thought the Monkey. But he kept his thoughts to himself, and only said: "Nothing could please me better than to be of service to Their Majesties. But it so happens that I left my liver

hanging on a branch of that big chestnut-tree, which you found me skipping about on. A liver is a thing that weighs a good deal. So I generally take it out and play about without it during the day-time. We must go back for it."

The Jelly-Fish agreed that there was nothing else to be done under the circumstances. For—silly creature that he was—he did not see that the Monkey was telling a story in order to avoid getting killed, and having his liver used as medicine for the fanciful young Queen.

When they reached the shore of Monkey-Land again, the Monkey bounded off the Jelly-Fish's back, and up to the topmost branch of the chestnut-tree in less than no time. Then he said: "I do not see my liver here. Perhaps somebody has taken it away. But I will look for it. You, meantime, had better go back and tell your Master what has happened. He might be anxious about you, if you did not get home before dark."

So the Jelly-Fish started off a second time; and when he got home, he told the Dragon King everything just as it had happened. But the King flew into a passion with him for his stupidity, and hallooed to his officers, saying:

"Away with this fellow! Take him, and beat him to a jelly! Don't let a single bone remain unbroken in his body!"

So the officers seized him, and beat him, as the King commanded. That is the reason why, to this very day, Jelly-Fishes have no bones, but are just nothing more than a mass of pulp.

As for the Dragon Queen, when she found she could not have the Monkey's liver—why! she made up her mind that the only thing to do was to get well without it.

The Death of Cleopatra

Antony and Cleopatra

WILLIAM SHAKESPEARE

Cleopatra. Give me my robe, put on my crown, I have
Immortal longings in me. Now no more
The juice of Egypt's grape shall moist this lip.
Yare, yare, good Iras; quick. Methinks I hear
Antony call: I see him rouse himself
To praise my noble act. I hear him mock
The luck of Caesar, which the gods give men
To excuse their after wrath. Husband, I come:
Now to that name my courage prove my title.
I am fire, and air; my other elements
I give to baser life. So, have you done?
Come then, and take the last warmth of my lips.
Farewell kind Charmian, Iras, long farewell.
Kisses them. Iras falls and dies.
Have I the aspic in my lips? Dost fall?
If thought and nature can so gently part,
The stroke of death is as a lover's pinch,
Which hurts, and is desired. Dost thou lie still?
If thus thou vanishest, thou tell'st the world
It is not worth leave-taking.

Charmian. Dissolve thick cloud, and rain, that I may say
The gods themselves do weep.
Cleopatra. This proves me base:
If she first meet the curled Antony,
He'll make demand of her, and spend that kiss
Which is my heaven to have. Come, though mortal wretch,
To an asp, which she applies to her breast
With thy sharp teeth this knot intrinsicate
Of life at once untie: poor venomous fool,
Be angry and despatch. O, couldst thou speak,
That I might hear thee call great Caesar ass
Unpolicied.
Charmian. O, eastern star.
Cleopatra. Peace, peace:
Dost thou not see my baby at my breast,
That suck the nurse asleep?
Charmian. O break! O break!
Cleopatra. As sweet as balm, as soft as air, as gentle.
O Antony! Nay, I will take thee too:
Applying another asp to her arm (dies)
What should I stay—

Charmian. In this vile world? So fare thee well:
Now boast thee, death, in thy possession lies
A lass unparallel'd. Downy windows close,
And golden Phoebus never be beheld
Of eyes again so royal: your crown's awry;
I'll mend it, and then play.

The Hair Tree

MARY DE MORGAN

Mary de Morgan was the sister of an important artist named William de Morgan. Important didn't mean he could ride about in a golden coach throwing silver coins to the poor. After a time, in fact, he gave up being an artist, because of his health, and became a writer. Before that, though, Lewis Carroll, who wrote about Alice, was one of the people who brought him work to do. Carroll ordered a set of tiles for a fireplace, and the tiles had to have on them the Mock Turtle and the Gryphon and other characters from Alice. *In the first edition of this story William de Morgan drew the pictures; but we have had new ones done. Mary was a lively girl, much too lively for her age when she was young, they thought in those days. She went on in the same way all her life, and finished by running a reform school in Egypt. You will find this a lively story, too. Whatever happens, though, you keep your hair on!*

W. M.

MANY years ago there lived a young Queen who was said to be the most beautiful woman in the world. Her skin was white and smooth as ivory, and her eyes bright as stars. But her greatest beauty was her hair. It was neither black nor gold, but exactly half-way between, just the colour of a dead beech-leaf. It was so long that it trailed behind her on the ground, and so thick that it took three maids to plait and arrange it every morning. Every day it was scented and washed by the court hairdresser, who examined it carefully to see that it was not growing thinner or falling off. The Queen's husband, the King, was as proud of it as his wife, and gave her all sorts of lovely jewellery with which to dress it—diamond pins and golden combs—and by his special command the court gardener always kept the best flowers for the Queen to place in her hair.

And not only the King and Queen, but all the courtiers and court ladies—indeed, everyone in the country—praised and admired this beautiful hair; and although some of the court ladies were rather jealous of it, yet all agreed that it would be a real national misfortune if any harm came to it.

One morning the Queen was sitting at her window at work, when a big bird flew past. It was much like an eagle, with a hooked beak and ugly fierce eyes. It hovered around the window for some time, and at last settled on a tree outside and watched the Queen, who did not look up till she was surprised by hearing the bird say in a harsh voice:

"Good day, Queen; you've plenty of hair."

The Queen laughed, well pleased that even a common eagle should notice her beautiful tresses.

"Yes," she said, shaking it around her. "I've more than any other lady in the land."

"Then you've enough to give me a little," said the bird. "I can't find anything soft to line my nest with, and some of your hair would do nicely."

"My hair!" cried the Queen, staring at the bird in astonishment. "My beautiful hair to line your common nest with! You must be mad. Do you know that I'm the Queen, and that I value my hair more than anything on earth?'"

"Nevertheless, it would do very nicely for my nest, and

I advise you to give me some of it," said the eagle in a threatening manner.

"Indeed, I shall do nothing of the kind," said the Queen, eagerly. "I never heard such impertinence in my life. Fly

away immediately, or I will send out some of the soldiers to shoot you."

"They couldn't do it," said the bird, with a low laugh; "and if you tell them to try, you will be sorry for it afterwards. Now, I shall only give you one more chance. Queen, will you give me some of your hair for my nest?"

"No, I shall not," answered the Queen, half crying with anger; "it is very presumptuous of you to ask for such a thing."

The bird said no more, but rising into the air began to fly slowly round and round the tree on which he had been perched, and as he flew he sang these words in a low voice;

"As the wind blows this tree's twigs bare,
So shall the proud Queen lose her hair;
The leaves shall come back with the first spring rain,
But when shall the Queen find her hair again?"

When he had done, the eagle gave a shrill cry and disappeared, leaving the Queen in astonishment at his conduct.

It was autumn, and she heard the wind whistling in the branches, and presently a number of leaves dropped from the cherry-tree, and fluttered to the ground, and, at the same moment, a handful of her curls fell out into her lap.

The Queen started up in alarm, and ran with tears in her eyes to the King to tell him what had happened. The King laughed at her fears, assuring her the bird could do her no harm, and that it was only by chance that her hair fell out just then.

Yet the Queen could not feel comfortable, and that night, when her ladies were brushing her hair, a quantity came out on the brushes and two or three locks fell to the ground. Next morning when she awoke she found some long soft brown tresses lying loose on her pillow, and when she got out of bed, a whole shower fell from her head to the floor.

The Queen wrung her hands in despair, and at once sent for the court hairdresser, who came, bringing with him a number of bottles, all containing lotions to make the hair grow; but all the lotions in the world were of no use. There was no denying the fact that the Queen's hair was falling out in a most alarming manner. There was scarcely enough for her ladies to plait, and a bald spot was beginning to show on the top of her head. She dared not look at the cherry-tree to see if its branches were beginning to look bare also, but at every gust she heard the leaves falling, and trembled as she thought how soon they would all be gone. At last one morning, after the wind had been very fierce and strong, she ran to the window, and, looking out, saw that the cherry-tree's branches were quite bare—not a leaf to be seen anywhere. Then she turned to her looking-glass, and, dreadful to behold, she was quite bald also. Her last lock of hair had fallen off and left her head as smooth and white as an egg. At this fearful sight the Queen screamed and fainted, and when her ladies came to help her they were all so shocked that they could scarcely speak. As for the King, his grief was so great that he sobbed aloud.

The Queen was laid on her bed, and the court physicians and hairdressers held a great consultation as to what was to be done to make her hair grow, and it was agreed that her head should go through a regular course of treatment. In the meantime she said she would keep to her room, and word was given out that she was very ill, in order that the common people might not know what a dreadful thing had happened. But all the doctors and hairdressers could do nothing. Not a single hair reappeared on the Queen's bare white head, and it was impossible to conceal the fact any longer. There was great sorrow all over the country when it became known, and a general mourning was proclaimed till the Queen's hair should have grown again. In the meantime she wore a little lace cap trimmed with jewels. It was a very pretty little cap, and very becoming—so, at

least, all the courtiers said. But it was not so beautiful as her own hair, and the Queen felt this so much that the first time she appeared in public in her cap she could scarcely help crying.

So things went on for a little time, and the doctors and hairdressers were all racking their brains to find something to make her hair grow. But the Queen fretted so much that she lost her appetite and really fell ill, and was obliged to keep to her bed. The first night after her illness she dreamt a dream, which she thought about all day long. She dreamt that she was sitting in the palace garden, when there came up a little man, who was the strangest object she had ever seen. He was no bigger than a big spider, and all dressed in green. When he saw her he began to dance and sing this rhyme:

> "When the grass is thin, you must mow it, mow it,
> mow it,
> But when the ground is bare, you must sow it, sow it,
> sow it."

And as he sang these words he took out a handful of tiny seeds from his pocket, and began to scatter them about. Directly there sprang up a little plant, which grew and grew and grew until it became a big tree, and then it put forth buds, and the buds burst, and there came out not leaves, but tiny locks of hair, which grew and grew until they touched the ground, and covered the tree all over.

When the Queen awoke she could think of nothing but the strange Hair Tree; and that night when she went to sleep she dreamt exactly the same thing. On the third night she had the same dream again, and when she awoke she called to her husband, and told him of what she had dreamt three nights running.

"And now, my dear husband," she continued, "I am sure that the only thing which can ever make my hair grow is some seeds from the Hair Tree. I entreat you to spare no effort to discover it, and to offer a reward to anyone who will bring you news of it. For I feel"—here the Queen's voice grew very husky—"that if I do not find it I shall never recover my hair, and if not, I shall die, for I cannot live without it." So saying she fell back on the pillow and closed her eyes.

The King at once called his Privy Council together, and he told them the Queen's dream. A herald was sent round to proclaim that one hundred thousand pounds would be given to anyone who could bring some seeds from the Hair Tree, or even tell where it was to be found. And great posters were pasted up all over the kingdom, offering the reward. So everyone began to talk of this strange Hair Tree, which no one had ever heard of before, and to wonder where it could be—for all would have liked to have earned the reward—but all agreed that the Hair Tree was nowhere in that country.

Now it chanced that a poor sailor named Rupert saw one of the placards, and stopped to read it. He was a strong young man, but he had neither father nor mother, nor sisters nor brothers, and he felt so lonely that he did not care what became of him. So when he saw the placard and the large reward that was offered to anyone who could bring news of the Hair Tree, he began to wonder where it was, and if he could not find it.

"One hundred thousand pounds is a lot of money," he said to himself. "There is no reason why I should not find it as well as another man. I have a good mind to go and look for it, though it seems rather a wild-goose chase."

So he packed up his things, and took a little boat, and

sailed away towards the north; for it was there, he knew, was a strange country where animals speak like men and women, and plants have hands and eyes; and he thought that there he might find the wonderful Hair Tree.

In the meantime half the young men in the kingdom had started off to search, hoping to win the reward. Some went east, some went west, some north, some south; and they sought in every imaginable place and country. Some gave it up very soon, and returned home, saying that there was no such tree. Others went on and on, asking everyone they met if they had heard of or seen it, and finding no trace of it, yet, being determined not to give it up and return home empty-handed, went still farther and farther. And so months passed away, and the Queen's head still remained bald.

In order that her Majesty might not be annoyed by the sight of other women's hair when her own was gone, the King ordered that they should all wear little caps which quite covered the head and came down on the forehead; and because no one liked these caps, and all thought them very unbecoming, the court ladies were almost as anxious as the Queen that the tree should be found, and her hair grow again.

Rupert sailed and sailed to the north till he began to think he must be coming to the magic country of which he had heard. For a long time he went on without seeing land anywhere, but at last he came in sight of a little island standing quite alone in the middle of the water. On it there grew neither grass nor flowers of any sort, but three solitary trees. One was much like a common nut-tree, only all the nuts were of a bright red colour; the boughs of the second were laden with precious stones of all kinds, diamonds and rubies, emeralds and pearls; but the third tree was the strangest of all, for its boughs were quite bare, and looked as if they were made of polished brass, and on the centre at the top grew an enormous pod, which pointed straight at the sky. It looked like a great brass drum.

Rupert pulled up his boat, and, springing on to the island, filled his pockets full of precious stones and common nuts, and then stood still looking at the enormous pod and wondering what it could contain. While he watched it there was a noise like a clap of thunder, and the pod burst asunder, and twelve round shining golden nuts fell to the ground. At the same time the tree withered as if it had been struck by lightning, and the brass branches all fell away.

Rupert was so frightened by the noise the pod made in bursting that he had buried his face in the ground, but when he found all was quiet again, he slowly raised himself, and picked up one of the gold nuts to examine it. As they were pretty and bright, he thought he would take them all for curiosities, and he placed them on the seat of his little boat. But as he rowed away from the island he began to feel sure he was coming to the enchanted land. The fishes no longer started away from the side of the boat, but swam after it in a long trail, and when he baited his line and threw it overboard not one would bite, but swam up quite close to the hook and then turned away, giving little low, scoffing laughs. Rupert was sorely puzzled, and sat looking at the water in wonder, when he heard a whirring of wings overhead, and a great yellow bird flew round the boat, and at last perched on the prow and peered curiously into his face.

After a few minutes it said, "Are those nuts you have in your pocket?"

Rupert said, "Yes," and drawing out a handful of the red nuts, offered them to the bird.

"Crack some and give me the kernels," said the bird. Rupert obeyed, afraid to refuse, as he remembered what a dreadful thing had happened to the poor Queen for not being polite to a bird. The bird went on eating the nuts, and then said:

"Where are you going?"

Then the sailor told how the Queen had been rude to a bird, who had in return destroyed her hair.

"I know; that was me," said the bird, with a chuckle. "Give me some more nuts."

Rupert again handed the bird the nuts, and then went on relating how the Queen had had a strange dream of a wonderful Hair Tree, and how the King had offered a reward to anyone who could find it; so he was going to look for it.

"You will search a long time for the Hair Tree, I expect," said the bird, still munching. "If the Queen waits for her hair till it is found, she will have to do without it nearly all her life. I suppose she'll wish now that she had been civil." But as he finished speaking, the bird's glance fell on the golden nuts lying on the seat, and with a shrill cry he flew at them; but Rupert had seized them first and held them firmly out of his reach.

"What are these?" gasped the bird. "Where did you get them? Tell me at once."

"They came," said Rupert, still holding the bag tightly, "from the single pod of a tree that has no leaves, and whose branches look like brass, and that grows on a little island not far from here." On hearing this the bird gave a low cry, and crouched down on one side of the boat, where it sat eyeing Rupert and the nuts greedily, and shaking with

rage. "Then they are the nuts of the zirbal-tree," he said at last; "and the pod has broken when I was not there. For two thousand years I have waited for that pod to break, and now it will be two thousand years before it is ripe again, and it is the only zirbal-tree living, and there is nothing on earth like its nuts."

When Rupert saw the bird crouched in one corner of the seat, with its head lowered and its feathers ruffled, and remembered how much mischief it had done, he felt strongly inclined to seize it and wring its neck, but he restrained himself and said:

"You had better sit up. I've got the nuts, and I mean to keep them; but perhaps, if you'll answer me one or two questions, I'll give you one."

On this the bird drew itself up, and, arranging its ruffled plumage, sat watching Rupert suspiciously.

"You say you're the bird who charmed away the Queen's hair. Well, if you'll tell me how she can grow it again, I'll give you a nut."

"What!" cried the bird, flapping his wings angrily. "Tell you how the Queen can recover her hair? Never—I'd sooner never taste a nut again."

"Very well," said Rupert, picking up a golden nut, and holding it temptingly towards the bird. "Only tell me which way I ought to steer to find the country where the Hair Tree grows, and I will give you this."

The bird sat silent, with his head on one side, watching Rupert for some time, and then with a sudden cry rose into the air and was out of sight almost before he knew it had moved.

At first he felt angry at this, but as it was gone, it was no use thinking about it, and, anyhow, he had learnt that the golden nuts were very valuable, and he thought if it wanted them so much it might perhaps return for them.

He was right. All day and night he drifted about without coming in sight of land, but next morning at sunrise he saw, in the far distance, a dim line, and at the same moment he heard a whirring of wings overhead, and the eagle flew down and perched on the edge of the boat as before.

Rupert remained quiet, without seeming to notice it, until at last it broke silence with:

"Are you in the same mind as last night? I'll tell you the way to the Hair Tree country for a zirbal nut."

The sailor took one out of his pocket and said:

"Tell me first, then, and you shall have the nut afterwards."

"That is the country where the Hair Tree grows, in front of you," said the bird. "Many go to it, but very few return."

"Why is that?" asked Rupert, as he gave the bird the nut.

"Why?" repeated the bird, seizing it with his bill. "You had better go there and find out. You know now where it is."

Rupert pondered a little; then he said: "If you will tell me how to find my way safely to the Hair Tree and back, when I pass here again I will give you six whole nuts. And if you refuse I shall take my gun and shoot you."

The bird gave a scornful laugh. "You couldn't shoot me," he said; "you can try if you like. Why, if it were not for the magic fruit in your pocket, you wouldn't be here now. It is only that which has protected you from my spells. Well, perhaps I will do what you want, and tell you how to find your way to the Hair Tree; only, you must promise faithfully to give me the nuts when you return."

The sailor promised again, and the bird continued:

"When you reach land you can go on shore at any place—it doesn't matter where—and walk straight on. You will find that all the animals can speak; but I advise you not to speak to any of them. And, whatever you do, beware of the plants and flowers; for they all have hands and arms, and will try to seize you, and if once they get you nothing can save you—no, not even your magic nuts. You must go on till you come to a high wall, in which is a heavy iron door, over which is written:

"Only he who knows can enter here.
Yet only he can know, who enters without fear."

And you must stand before it, and say:

"I know, I know
Inside the wind does blow,
Inside the waters flow;
This makes the Hair Tree grow—
I know, I know."

Then the doors will fly open, and you can pass in. Within grows the Hair Tree. What else you will find there, I shall not say. Now, I have kept my part of the agreement; see that you keep yours when you return."

So saying, the bird flapped his wings once and disappeared.

Rupert looked about, and finding himself very near land, rowed to shore, and stepped from his boat. It seemed to be a pretty sort of country, and at first he did not notice anything unusual. He walked straight on till he came to a row of splendid sunflowers, and stopped in front of them to admire them, when all at once a pair of beautiful white hands and arms were thrust out from the nearest stalk, and grasping him by the shoulders began to pull him with a strength he could not resist. At once all the other stalks had put out their hands, and were reaching towards him. And from above the large yellow flowers there appeared heads—women's heads—with beautiful dreamy faces and bright golden hair. In another moment Rupert felt the arms would have crushed him to death, for they were fast tightening their hold, and felt like iron bands.

Suddenly he remembered the jewels in his pocket, and drawing out a brilliant emerald, flashed it before the face of the sunflower in whose arms he was.

"Leave me alone," he cried, "and you shall have this."

But still the arms bound him with their strong grasp, and gave no sign of loosening their hold. Then Rupert took the jewel and, holding it above his head, said, "If you don't let me go at once, I will throw it beyond your reach, so that you will never get it."

For a moment the arms wavered, then they slowly gave way, and Rupert burst from them trembling at the danger from which he had escaped. With haste, and still keeping at arm's length, he dropped the jewel into the cruel beautiful white hand that was stretched out to receive it. Then he ran as fast as he could from the row of sunflowers and sat down, still panting and trembling, on a large bare stone.

After he had a little recovered himself, he looked about him, and perceived that not only the sunflowers but all the trees had hands and arms, which they were always stretching to try and catch something, and on looking on the ground he saw that even the blades of grass were armed with tiny hands, which they kept stretching into the air.

For amusement he buried his hand in the grass, and in an instant it was clutched by a hundred tiny hands, that pulled it hard. He could easily draw it away, for it was no more than if a number of spiders had seized his hand. He wondered much at this country, where all the plants seemed to be alive, and he had seen no trace of man or beast. While he was thinking, a shadow fell across his path, and looking up he saw a large handsome tigress standing in front of him looking into his face. He at once put his hand to his gun, and would have shot it if it had not said in a quiet voice:

"Why are you going to shoot me? I shall do you no harm. How did you come here? You are the first man who has been on this island since I came."

Rupert stared in astonishment at hearing a tigress speak so plainly and said:

"I came in a little boat. My name is Rupert, and I am come to look for the Hair Tree. Who are you? I never heard a tigress speak before."

"I am not really a tigress; I am a woman who was turned into a tigress by a wicked fairy. Tell me what you want with the Hair Tree, and how you managed to get here alive, and I will tell you my story."

So Rupert told the tigress all that had happened to him; how he had set out to find the Hair Tree, and how he had picked up the nuts of the zirbal-tree, and his promise to the yellow bird, and how he had only just escaped from the sunflowers.

She listened quietly; then she said, "You owe your life to the nuts of the zirbal-tree. They are enchanted, and that is why the yellow eagle could not kill you at once, as he would otherwise have done, for he is a most spiteful creature, but the magic nuts saved you from him, as well as from a number of dangers of this island of which you do not know. You are the first living man who has ever entered so far. Now let us sit down, and keep well out of reach of the grasping hands, and I will tell you my story."

Rupert sat down, and the tigress arranged herself at his feet, and curled her tail beneath her, and began as follows:

The Story of Trevina

My name was Trevina. I was the youngest of three sisters, and my father was a miller. I was the most beautiful of the three. We lived in a mill on the bank of a river, close by the sea, and my greatest amusement was to search about on the rocks for the strange animals and seaweed I found there.

A little way in the sea was a small island, on which great sea-birds collected but where we never went, as there was nothing to be got there, and it was difficult to climb on it, for it was surrounded by sharp rocks. Nevertheless I often looked at it, and wondered what sort of a place it was, and thought I would try to get to it when I could.

One evening as I was walking along the shore, I noticed that I was followed by a large tortoise, who kept close to me, and looked up into my face beseechingly. I did not think it odd, for there were plenty of tortoises among the rocks, and when they were hungry they often followed us, hoping for food. But when I got home I found the same tortoise in my room, and not liking to send away a creature who kept so close to me, I gave it some bread and milk, and a little bit of matting to sleep on. My sisters laughed at me for my new pet, but nevertheless I took great care of my tortoise, and let it follow me where it liked. After a time, however, its affection for me became quite tiresome. I could not move without its following me closely, and even if I fell asleep and woke I found it sitting watching me. I began to feel provoked with it, and declared that if it continued to be so worrying I would take it and throw it into the sea. Would that I had, alas!

My father owned a boat on the river, and often on hot afternoons I would step into it, and lie there, idly gazing at the sky and enjoying the rippling motion, and as it was always safely moored to the side I felt no fear of drifting away.

On one unlucky afternoon I went out about sunset, and placed myself comfortably in the cushions at the bottom of the boat, meaning to spend an hour in reading. But I was overcome with the heat, and ere I had been there long fell fast asleep. I slept soundly, and when I awoke I found that it was getting quite dark. Starting up, I saw with terror that the boat was no longer in the river, but had been evidently loosed from its fastenings and had drifted to sea, and was already half way to the island. I did not know that the tortoise had followed me, but looking on the seat I saw it sitting there, and I felt a positive hatred for it when I saw the salf-satisfied leer with which it was regarding me. To my fright and astonishment, it drew near to me, and with a deep bow said:

"Be not astonished, lovely Trevina, and be assured that no harm shall come to you. Know that I am no common tortoise, but am the king of the tortoises, and only for your sake have assumed the shape of a common animal, in order that I might dwell near you. I have loved you from the first moment I saw you, and now intend to make you my wife. When we arrive at the island, where my armies are waiting for me, I shall appear in my proper form. Resistance on your part will be useless. From here no one can hear your cries, and as soon as we reach the island my people will bore a hole in the bottom of the boat and sink it, so your return will be impossible. After a day or two I shall transport you to my own home. I should do so at once, were it not that I fear the jealousy of my mother, who wishes me to marry the snake-princess."

I scarcely could hear him to the end with patience. Starting up, I tried to seize him in my hands, meaning to throw him into the water, and so rid myself of his impertinence; but the moment I touched him his whole shape began to change, and swell, and he was quickly transformed into the most hideous figure I had ever beheld. It was like a little grey man not more than two feet high, and it carried on its back an enormous shell, while its arms and legs were exactly like those of an immense tortoise. And its face. I shudder even now when I remember how hideous it was. The great glaring eyes, the huge mouth, the hideous shrivelled skin! I screamed aloud with all my might, hoping my father or sisters might hear, and, turning my face, covered my eyes with my hands, that they might not be annoyed by the sight of the disgusting creature. But all my shrieks were vain, my voice was blown away by the wind, and no answer came from the shore. On thus seeing my distress my tormentor only laughed.

Gradually the boat sailed to the island, and on looking up I saw that it was covered with tortoises of all sizes, evidently awaiting our arrival. I think I must have fainted. Anyhow, I remember nothing more till I found myself lying on my back in the middle of the island, surrounded by tortoises, and their hideous king leaning tenderly over me. I started up and, bursting through their lines, ran down to the water's edge, but finding there no means of escape, I flung myself on the ground crying and sobbing. I felt sure that in time my father and sisters would miss me, and come to the island to search for me, but the notion of being left alone with my horrid tortoise lover till they could come was dreadful. All that night I sat upon a rock close by the water's edge, weeping bitterly, but still feeling quite sure that in the morning I should see my father coming for me; but morning came and he did not appear, and the day passed away, and still he did not come, and when evening came round again, I began to fear I must give myself up, and had determined that, rather than listen to the odious tortoise-king, I would throw myself into the water, and so put an end to my life. I was standing upon a rock looking into the clear green water, and thinking whether I would wait another day or spring into it at once, and so end my troubles, when I heard a soft voice above me saying, "Trevina," and looking up, I saw a beautiful sea-gull floating in the air.

"Poor Trevina," he said, "I can't carry you away, but I can take a message to your father. I hate the tortoise-king and his mother as much as you do, and would gladly do anything to annoy them. Tell me what I shall say to your father, and I will fly to him tonight."

"Will you really, dear, dear gull?" I cried, joyfully. "I shall be grateful to you all my life. Go, then, and tell him that I was stolen by the tortoise-king, and am upon the little island. Tell him to come for me at once, and to bring plenty of guns and swords with which to kill the tortoises."

But scarcely were the words out of my mouth when there was a rumbling noise beside me, and with a bang like thunder a gulf opened in the ground, and there started up through it a hideous figure, very much like the tortoise-king, but bigger and fatter, whom I at once guessed to be his mother. The sea-gull, at first sight of her, gave a shrill cry and flew away.

"So, girl," she cried, in a dreadful voice, "not content

with rejecting my son's noble offers, you would try to put an end to his life. It is lucky, indeed, for him that, with a mother's care, I have been watching him and you, when he thought me far away. I was sure no good would come of it, when he honoured you, a common human being, with his love, instead of offering it, as I wished, to the snake-princess. But now you shall be punished. Bitterly may you regret your unfeeling conduct."

At this moment I saw the tortoise-king coming in haste towards us, waddling as fast as his little short legs and heavy shell would let him.

He turned to his mother, and, falling on his knees before her, tried to calm her rage—but in vain. She continued, more fiercely than before:

"Yes! You shall be well punished, for you shall become a tigress; and, left by yourself in the enchanted land, you will wish you had been grateful to my son for his kindness in offering to make you his wife." Then she waved her grey hands in the air, and I felt a dreadful change coming upon me. Hair was growing all over me. My arms became forelegs like those of a tiger. I felt a tail beginning to sprout out behind.

"And now," cried the tortoise-queen, her eyes sparkling with spiteful pleasure, "you may be very thankful if you remain in your present condition; but if you eat only one mouthful of flesh, you will become a real tigress, and then you can never regain your proper form. As it is, the only way by which you can ever recover your own shape is by being beaten by a man with the rods that grow beneath the Hair Tree."

I could not speak; I tried, but my voice was choked with tears. I clasped my hands, but found that they would not close on account of the claws which were growing at the ends. I threw myself on the ground at the Queen's feet to beg for mercy, but I was not allowed to remain long, for, taking me by the nape of my neck, she carried me quickly through the air, and did not stop till we reached this island, where she flung me on the ground with a spiteful laugh, and vanished. For some time I lay in silent misery, till roused by the voice of the sea-gull calling me by name, and raising myself, I saw it hovering over me.

"Poor Trevina," he said mournfully, "you are worse off now than you were before; but keep a good heart. You will some time recover your proper form, I feel sure; but be sure you eat nothing but herbs."

I thanked the sea-gull, and tried to feel more cheerful; but my case seemed a hard one, for how was ever any man to come to this enchanted ground? and if anyone did get so far, I knew there must be great difficulty in getting the rods from the Hair Tree.

You are the first man I have seen since I was brought here; and since that time I have lived on grass and herbs. Every day have I wept afresh at the thought that I should never again see my dear home or my father and sisters; and my joy, therefore, on seeing you knew no bounds.

*

As she finished, the tigress turned on one side to wipe away a tear, and Rupert was scarcely less moved than she by the story of her misfortunes.

"But how can I help you, poor Trevina?" said he, after a pause.

"Help me!" cried the tigress, her eyes sparkling with joy. "Are you not searching for the Hair Tree, and do not the rods with which I am to be beaten grow around it?

Dear, kind sailor, you will surely not refuse to pick one and beat me with it."

Rupert, of course, could not refuse to do as she asked, but the thought of having to beat her filled him with disgust. After a pause she arose, and bade him do the same.

"Now," she said, "it is time for you to continue your journey. I cannot go with you farther, but you must continue straight ahead, turning neither to the right nor left, and take the greatest care you can of the zirbal nuts, for they are the best protection you can have against every sort of spell. You will find me here on your return, but be sure you do not forget to bring with you some of the rods which grow underneath the Hair Tree."

Rupert promised, and said adieu, and went on his way; but he was so full of thoughts of poor Trevina and her sorrows that he had almost forgotten the Queen's hair and the reward, and was more anxious to find the wonderful Hair Tree, that he might beat the tigress with the rods he found there, than to gather the hair seeds for the Queen.

As he went on he found the path growing narrower and narrower, and the rocks on each side grew larger and larger, and began to arch over the top of the path, and to darken it. All round the wind moaned piteously, and from afar he could hear a sound like running water. At last he came to a place where the rocks blocked up the path, and in them he perceived a small door. He pushed it open, and stepped through into a long dark narrow passage, down which he walked. Presently a faint light became visible, and after a time he found himself in front of a high wall, so high that he could not see to the top, in which was a gate on which was written in letters of gold:

"Only he who knows can enter here.
Yet only he can know, who enters without fear."

Then Rupert remembered what the bird had said, and stood in front of the gate and said:

"I know, I know
Inside the wind doth blow,
Inside the waters flow;
This makes the Hair Tree grow—
I know, I know."

In a moment the door flew open, and Rupert stepped inside and looked about him.

He found himself standing at the beginning of a long flat tract of country, but for a moment or two he was so dazzled by the light which enveloped everything that he could scarcely see.

This light was quite unlike anything he had ever seen; it was of a pale clear green colour, and as his eyes grew a little more used to it, he perceived that it filled every nook and corner, and the only shade anywhere was thrown by the black rays of a black sun in the sky!

It was very strange. He rubbed his eyes and looked again, but there it was sure enough. The sun was coal black, and threw out long black rays, while everywhere else was light.

A little in front was a black river flowing around an island, in the centre of which was a mound where grew a tree—such a tree! At sight of it Rupert's heart gave a great bound, and he felt as if he would go mad with joy, for he knew when he saw it he had come to the end of his journey. On that tree grew no leaves, but it was covered with soft fine hair, which grew from all its branches and fell in waves to the ground. He could not see it very plainly, for the river was wide, but he saw that the island was covered with plants of various kinds. He sat down on the pebbly bank of the river, gazing across and wondering if the water were deep, or how he should manage to cross to the other side. While he was sitting thinking he put his hand into his pocket and drew out a zirbal nut. Just as he was looking at it, he heard a rippling of the water, and perceived an immense swan swimming along towards him. It was as large as a horse, and brilliant yellow all over, with eyes of shining red that shot out sparks of fire. Rupert sprang back from the bank, for the swan appeared to be very angry, and called out in an awful voice:

"What man are you? And what do you do here so near the magic Hair Tree?"

"My name is Rupert," said the sailor, trembling in every limb, "and I mean no harm; I only wish to gather some of the seeds to bring back the Queen's hair. I should be much obliged to you if you will tell me how to get over the water, and if it's deep."

The swan did not answer, but its eyes were fixed on the nut in Rupert's hand, which it was eyeing greedily.

"What have you there?" it said, after a pause, in a much quieter voice. "Surely that is a zirbal nut. Dear me, it is two thousand years since I tasted one. Give me a bit of that one."

"I am sure you are very welcome to it," Rupert was beginning, but he stopped himself in time, and said instead:

"If you will take me on your back across the river, and wait for me and bring me back after I have got some hair seeds, I will give you this one, but on no other condition."

The swan stopped, and thought, and then said, "Very well"; and swimming close to the bank, beckoned to Rupert to get on his back. He obeyed, and the swan swam swiftly over the water. As it approached the farther side, it turned its long head and said:

"Whatever you do, don't let the lip-flowers kiss you. They are sure to ask to. But they won't really want to kiss. They will only bite a piece out of your cheek; they are terribly greedy."

The sailor thanked the swan for its advice, and sprang upon the mound. It was covered with plants bearing such flowers as man had never seen before. Some of them were like mouths—soft red lips folded over the whitest rows of shining teeth; and when Rupert struck one of them by chance, they gave a loud angry cry, whilst all the others burst into such weird laughter that he thought it dreadful to hear. But one and all, as he passed by them, swayed their long stalks towards him, and said, "Let me give you a kiss—only one: let me kiss your cheek." But he minded what the swan had said, and, keeping carefully out of their reach, turned to examine the other flowers. Some were like delicate waxen ears, and these, with their dark green leaves, he did not think at all ugly. But the prettiest of all grew on long slender stalks, and bent like lilies, and their flowers were like human eyes. Big eyes, small eyes, blue eyes, brown eyes, black eyes, hazel eyes, eyes with long black lashes, eyes with scarcely any, eyes with heavy lids—all sorts of eyes, all looking curiously at him. He thought them so pretty that he determined to gather some, and on coming to a very beautiful bright blue eye, he put his hand to the stalk to break it off, but thereupon it wept such floods of tears that the sailor felt sorry for it, and left it glistening on its stem, whereat all the lips burst into a chorus of shrill laughter. But now he was nearing the wonderful Hair Tree, and could think of nothing else. All round it grew a double row of dark green plants, with long stiff leaves, from whose centres grew tall solid silver rods in the place where flowers should be. These rods stood

so near together that they made a quite compact railing around the Hair Tree, and it was impossible to get to it without passing through their line.

Drawing close to them, the sailor examined them carefully, to see where they could be gathered, for doubtless these were the rods of which Trevina spoke. They seemed to be fastened into the plants with a sort of hinge, and beneath this Rupert took hold of one to break it off, but no sooner had he begun to pull, than the rod, swinging on its joint, dealt him a smart blow on the face, which made him stagger back, and all the lip-flowers laughed again.

"Oh! zirbal nuts," he cried, taking one from his pocket, "you have helped me before, help me again." No sooner had he spoken than all the lips cried out, "A nut, a nut—give us a nut!"

Then a beautiful rosy mouth, growing on a very tall

stalk, turned to the others and called, "Silence!" and bending towards Rupert said, "Listen; take out your penknife and cut that nut in pieces, and give them to us, and we will bite off some of the silver rods for you, so that you can pass through to the Hair Tree."

Rupert agreed, and taking out his penknife began to chop up the nut, whilst a number of mouths turned themselves to the silver rods and began to bite their stalks. It was vain for the rods to slash about, they could not hurt the lip-flowers, who went on steadily gnawing till half a dozen rods lay on the ground leaving a clear path through to the Hair Tree.

Rupert at once gave the pieces of nut to the mouths (which opened greedily to receive them), and walked up to the tree and stood beneath it.

What a wonderful tree it was! The hair rippled down from all its branches, and was of all colours—black outside, and growing lighter and lighter till, quite near the trunk, it was of fine pure gold. Rupert took hold of it and passed it though his fingers.

How soft and thick it felt! What would not the court ladies have given for even a tiny branch of it! Then he thought of the Queen's hair, and turned to look for the seeds.

He found them in little pods growing close to the branches and at once tried to pull them off. But he found that they grew on hairs so long and thick that he had to take out his knife and cut them, and even then it was a long time before he could gather any quantity. At last he succeeded in picking a handful, and, wrapping them carefully in his handkerchief, placed them in his bosom. When he turned to go, the eye-flowers had all closed, and were evidently fast asleep; the lips, too, were shut and still, and said nothing as he passed them. The black sun was fast sinking, and the black rays had become longer and darker. Rupert walked quickly down to where the yellow swan was waiting, carrying the silver rods with him.

"Make haste," said the swan. "What a long time you've been! It's getting quite light, and I want to go to sleep."

"To sleep!" said the sailor, staring. "Why, one goes to sleep when it gets dark, one wakes when it's light."

"Does one?" said the swan, scornfully. "That would be very foolish; where would be the use of going to sleep, and shutting one's eyes in the dark? The dark never hurts anyone's eyes. Of course one shuts one's eyes when it's too light, and it would hurt one to keep them open."

Rupert was silent, not knowing what to say, and the swan swam with him quickly across the water.

"Now," he said, as he landed him on the other side, "give me my nut, and take my advice, go away as quickly as you can. It's getting so light that soon you won't be able to see anything for the glare."

Rupert obeyed, and turned at once to go back, for a dull glaring light was beginning to spread everywhere as the black sun sank, and no sooner had it disappeared than the light became so intense that he could scarcely see, and had to shade his eyes with his hands as he felt his way to the door in the wall. This time no speech on his part was necessary, for it stood wide open, though it shut with a loud bang as soon as he had passed through it. He walked as quickly as he could down the long dark passage, and out into the broad daylight again, and there he sat down to think over all the strange things he had seen. He would have believed it all a dream, but for the seeds in his bosom and the rods at his side. And there, just as he had left them, were the long rows of sunflowers with the beautiful faces looking over their tops, and the white arms and hands stretching out from their sides; and then, after a few minutes, he saw the tigress coming towards him, walking very slowly, as if she had scarcely strength to move, and looking very thin.

"At last you are come," she cried, when she saw him; "how long I have waited for you!"

"Long!" said Rupert, staring with surprise. "Why, I have not been gone many hours."

"Hours!" said the tigress feebly. "Why, you have been gone six months."

"Six months!" cried Rupert. "And it has seemed to me like two hours."

"But you have returned, and have brought the rod with you," she said, joyfully. "So now all is right. But I am very hungry, for I have not been able to find any grass or herbs for a week. So now make haste and beat me at once."

"Beat you, you poor starved creature!" cried the sailor, looking pityingly at her; "beat a poor thing who has scarcely strength to crawl! I wouldn't do such a thing for the world!"

"Beat me—beat me, I tell you," called the tigress, writhing on the ground in front of him. "Beat me at once, or it will be the worse for both of us." Then she added, in a terrible voice, "Did I not tell you I was very hungry? Beat me at once, or *I shall eat you!*"

On hearing this, Rupert made no more ado, but seizing the silver rod, began to thrash the tigress with all his might. She stood quite still to receive his blows, only every now and then urging him on by calling:

"Harder! Beat harder!"

Rupert obeyed and then, just as he was going to fling

aside the rod and declare he would beat no longer, her skin began to shrivel, and at last fell to the ground, and there arose from it the loveliest maiden Rupert had ever beheld. Her hair, of burning gold, was worthy of the Hair Tree itself, whilst her shining blue eyes and rosy lips were far more beautiful than the strange flowers that grew about it.

Rupert stood still staring at her in wonder, but she at once put out her hand and said, "How can I thank you enough for what you have done for me? I am Trevina. Now let us hurry away from this dreadful place as fast as we can, but first give me a nut to protect me from spells."

Rupert at once gave her one, and as she fastened it into the bosom of her dress, she turned to him and asked with a smile, "Am I like what you expected?"

"You are far, far more beautiful," answered he. "Is it really possible that you were that tigress?"

"I was indeed that tigress," said Trevina, as they began to walk quickly to the shore; "and should most likely have remained so but for you. As it is I shall not feel comfortable till we are off this dreadful island, although the zirbal nuts are the best protection we could have."

"Now, indeed, am I thankful that the Queen lost her hair," cried Rupert, "since it has helped me to set you free, lovely Trevina."

They soon found the little boat, and getting into it, sailed away as fast as they could.

After a little time Rupert remembered the bird and his promise, and said to Trevina that he supposed they should soon see him coming for his nuts.

"You have just eight nuts left, and you have promised the eagle six," said Trevina. "By all means give him the six you promised him, but let me entreat you to keep the

remaining two. One I have here, and be sure you do not let him have the other. Remember that the moment you have parted from it, he will have as much power over you as he had over the poor Queen. He will beg you for it, but he must not have it."

Rupert promised, and in a very short time they saw the eagle flying towards them. He flew round them in circles, and at last alighted on the prow of the boat.

"Well," he said, fiercely, looking towards Rupert, "I see you have the seeds. Now where are my nuts?"

"Here they are," said he, taking six from his pocket, and giving them to him. The eagle took them in his claws and hid them in his feathers, but still he did not go.

"You have yet got one more," he said. "What are you going to do with it? You do not eat zirbal nuts."

"I mean to keep it as a curiosity," answered the sailor.

"But what use will that be?" croaked the bird. "Will you not give it to me?"

"No, I can't do that," said Rupert. "You must be content with what you've got."

"In my nest at home," said the eagle, "I have seven little eaglets, and you have only given me six nuts to take to them. Will you not give me your other nut for my youngest eaglet?"

On hearing this the sailor fingered the nut in his pocket and looked at the bird, and was just going to give it to him, when Trevina laid her hand on his arm to stop him, and turning to the eagle said:

"It is no use your asking for the nut, for he will not give it to you. I know quite well that you have no little eaglets at home, that is all false, and that you only say it to get the nut from him."

Then the eagle turned, and, giving one fearful shriek,

rose into the air and flew away, and Rupert and Trevina never saw him more.

★

A whole year had passed away since the Queen had dreamt the strange dream, and still her head was bald; and no one could tell how to make the hair grow again. Men had sought far and wide. The King had sent messengers to every part of the world. All sorts of strange plants had been brought and stranger remedies suggested. But it was quite evident that no one had found the real Hair Tree.

The Queen had been ill for months, and now scarcely ever appeared in public. At last, when she had quite made up her mind that she would never recover her hair, she sent for the King, and told him that she was seriously thinking of shutting herself up for the rest of her life, and would only consent to appear again on the condition that he should order that all the women in the land should have their heads shaved, as well as wear caps like hers. The King, in great consternation, begged her to reconsider her decision, but she was firm, and as he could not bear the thought of parting with her, he at last consented to publish a proclamation ordering that all the women in the country, from the greatest duchess to the poorest beggar, were to have their heads shaved, in order that the Queen might not be annoyed by the sight of their hair.

Great was the anger and discontent with which this order was received, but the people dared not disobey the King, so after a great deal of grumbling they agreed to submit in silence, and a day was settled on which the shaving was to take place, for the Queen wished it to be performed in public.

At her suggestion the King had an immense scaffold put up in the market-place, and on it the court barber was to stand, whilst all the women, from the highest to the lowest, came before him in turn and had their heads shaved quite close. State seats were erected on one side, on which the King and Queen and court would sit to watch the shaving.

When all this was settled, the Queen grew as cheerful as possible. She said it was almost as good as having her own hair back again.

The different messengers whom the King had sent in search of the Hair Tree still kept returning, each one bringing with him some strange new plant, but nothing that could do the Queen any good; and thus the time passed till the shaving day came. All the streets were hung with black, and the chair in which the ladies were to sit to be shaved was hung with black also.

Early in the morning a great crowd had assembled, and then the King and Queen came down and took seats, and the shaving was to begin.

The crier took out his list of the ladies' names, and called out the first, which was that of a duchess who was quite young and very beautiful. She rose slowly from her seat, sobbing bitterly, and walked towards the black chair.

She was dressed in a long black serge dress, without any ornament, but her beautiful white neck and arms were bare, and over her shoulders to her waist rippled her bright soft brown hair. She looked so young and so miserable that there was a general groan at the idea that all her lovely locks must fall.

With a last sob, the duchess took her seat in the dreadful chair, and, closing her eyes, resigned herself to her fate. The barber sharpened his razor, and was just going to begin, whilst all held their breath from excitement, when a voice was heard crying "*Stop!*" and in a minute all saw a sailor rushing towards the scaffold, panting and out of breath, but holding out something in his right hand.

"*Stop!*" he shouted, as loudly as he could, directly he found breath to speak. "I have got it—the hair seeds from the *real Hair Tree*!"

On hearing this the barber flung away his razor, and the Queen screamed outright.

The courtiers and the King danced a jig for joy, whilst the duchess who was to have been shaved, threw her arms round the sailor's neck, and kissed him at once.

"Only try," cried Rupert, eagerly, "before you shave them; they came from the Hair Tree. I picked them myself."

On hearing this, the Queen unable to contain her impatience any longer, dashed through the crowd, and pushing the duchess on one side, sprang into the black chair herself.

"There is no time like the present," she cried, pulling off her muslin cap, and flinging it to the ground, quite heedless of showing her bare shining head to the crowd. "Put some on yourself, dear sailor, and let us see how they do."

A thrill of excitement ran through the crowd, whilst, amid a dead silence, Rupert opened the packet, and carefully and slowly sprinkled the seeds over the Queen's bent head. In a moment a soft fine down began to appear all over it, growing thicker and darker every moment, till it was curly hair, which grew longer and longer as they watched it.

"How does it do?" gasped the Queen. "My head feels very queer. Is it growing?" But she had little need to ask the question, for no sooner were the words out of her mouth than the soft curly locks, of her own old colour,

fell over her shoulders, and grew till they reached her feet. At sight of them she shrieked with joy, and fainted, whilst the King and courtiers and all the crowd shouted and hurrahed as if they had gone mad.

That night the city was illuminated, and there was a great ball at the palace, and next day the King and Queen and all the court went to witness the wedding of Rupert and Trevina, after which the King presented Rupert with the reward.

One of his remaining nuts Rupert gave to the King to hang over the palace door, to defend them from all charms of bad fairies; but the other he and Trevina always kept, which is perhaps the reason they lived so happily together all the rest of their lives.

Our Lady's Mountebank

ANONYMOUS

In Our Lady's Litany the Virgin Mary is called the Queen of Angels, of Patriarchs, of Prophets and Apostles, of Martyrs, Confessors, Virgins and all Saints. And she is called the Queen of Peace. When I read this story I like to think she may also be called the Queen of humble innocent Mountebanks, (the old-fashioned name for jugglers).

E.F.

A MOUNTEBANK, who had become famous throughout France for his wonderful tumbling and juggling, grew very tired of his wandering life. At the end of each succeeding summer he found himself a little more oppressed by the noise and bustle of the world and a little more weary of his constant travelling from town to town. One very wet and windy day at the end of the harvest season, he came to the great monastery of Clairvaux. The kindly monks were much amused by his clever tricks, and when his performance was finished did not fail to point out to him the great difference between their life and his, which, being a clever fellow, he could see very well for himself. He told them he had in his wallet a goodly fortune made by his profession, and would give it all to our Lord and His Holy Mother if he might spend the rest of his life in the monastery. The Abbot, being appealed to, counted the contents of the wallet, and said it

was evidently the will of God that they should welcome this worthy man.

So the tumbler was dressed as a monk, and he soon began to accommodate himself to his new life. The order and discipline of the monastery gave him a pleasant feeling of security, and when he worked in the garden his heart was full of peace. But, as time went on, he began to feel sorrowful because his service was so poor. While the monks were busy chanting or praying or adding something more to their great learning, he was doing things of small importance to our Lord and His Holy Mother.

One day, being quite overcome by these troubling thoughts, he threw aside his spade, and, running down the steps into the crypt, fell on his knees before the image of the Virgin which was still standing on an old disused altar. There he poured out his pitiful tale, which simply amounted to this—that he loved the Holy Mother very dearly but had nothing worthy to give her. When he had finished this lamentation he was about to depart without feeling much relief, when he heard a Gentle Voice say, "Give what you have!"

"Ah!" exclaimed the mountebank, speaking to himself (for there was no one else to be seen). "Alas! I have nothing at all, for my little fortune is no longer mine." Having thus spoken, he was turning away, when he heard the Gentle Voice saying the same words as before. He stood still in front of the old altar for a long time, thinking very hard. And suddenly he remembered that he had one thing left—his wonderful art.

He threw off his long monkish robe, and, having freed his arms and legs from all restrictive coverings, he performed in front of the image of the Virgin all those mirth-provoking turns and tumbles which had so often delighted crowds of admiring spectators.

One of the monks finding the tumbler's spade in the garden raised a great alarm that the Devil had carried him off. The Abbot and the monks began a long search, which ended in the crypt, where they found the pious mountebank still leaping and tumbling before the altar. As the

Abbot was about to exclaim against this sacrilege, the poor man fell on the floor quite exhausted by the now unwonted exercise. Then a great miracle happened, for the Holy Virgin herself appeared, surrounded with a bright company of angels, and bending over the prostrate tumbler fanned his face with a little kerchief that she had.

The mountebank finished his life, as he had wished, in the monastery of Clairvaux, and when the end of it came it was not the Devil who carried his soul away but the Madonna herself and her bright company of angels.

Oh Sleep! it is a gentle thing
Beloved from pole to pole!
To Mary Queen the praise be given!
She sent the gentle sleep from Heaven,
That slid into my soul.

Samuel Taylor Coleridge.
From *The Rime of the Ancient Mariner*

How to Behave at Court

Miss Fanny Burney, the young authoress of Evelina, *is introduced by her friend, Mrs. Delaney to the Court of Queen Charlotte at Windsor.*

Windsor, Dec. 17th, 1785

My dearest Hetty,

I am sorry I could not more immediately write; but I really have not had a moment since your last.

Now I know what you next want is to hear accounts of kings, queens, and such royal personages. O ho! do you so? Well.

Shall I tell you a few matters of fact?—or, had you rather a few matters of etiquette? Oh, matters of etiquette, you cry! for matters of fact are short and stupid, and anybody can tell, and everybody is tired of them.

Very well, take your own choice. . . .

You would never believe—you, who distant from courts and courtiers, know nothing of their ways—the many things to be studied, for appearing with a proper propriety before crowned heads. Heads without crowns are quite other sort of rotundas.

Now, then, to the etiquette. I inquired into every particular, that no error might be committed. And as there is no saying what may happen in this mortal life, I shall give you those instructions I have received myself, that, should you find yourself in the royal presence, you may know how to comport yourself.

Directions for coughing, sneezing, or moving, before the King and Queen.

In the first place, you must not cough. If you find a cough tickling your throat, you must arrest it from making any sound; if you find yourself choking with the forbearance, you must choke—but not cough.

In the second place, you must not sneeze. If you have a vehement cold, you must take no notice of it; if your nose-membranes feel a great irritation, you must hold your breath; if a sneeze still insists upon making its way, you must oppose it, by keeping your teeth grinding together; if the violence of the repulse breaks some blood-vessel, you must break the blood-vessel—but not sneeze.

In the third place, you must not, on any account, stir either hand or foot. If, by chance, a black pin runs into your head, you must not take it out. If the pain is very great, you must be sure to bear it without wincing; if it brings the tears to your eyes, you must not wipe them off; if they give you a tingling by running down your cheeks, you must look as if nothing was the matter. If the blood should gush from your head by means of the black pin, you must let it gush; if you are uneasy to think of making such a blurred appearance, you must be uneasy, but you must say nothing about it. If, however, the agony is very great, you may, privately, bite the inside of your cheek, or of your lips, for a little relief; taking care, meanwhile, to do it so cautiously as to make no apparent dent outwardly. And, with that precaution, if you even gnaw a piece out, it will not be minded, only be sure either to swallow it, or

to commit it to a corner of the inside of your mouth till they are gone—for you must not spit.

I have many other directions, but no more paper; I will endeavour however, to have them ready for you in time.

Believe me, my dearest Esther,

Most affectionately yours,

F.B.

NOTE: Miss Fanny must have carried out these instructions up to the hilt; for Their Majesties were charmed with her, and soon afterwards Queen Charlotte appointed her to the coveted post of Mistress of the Wardrobe.

Mistresses of the Robes

VARIOUS

What Queens Wore

I

The Empress Eugénie of France, on her Marriage to the Emperor Napoleon the Third in 1853

Her long-trained bridal gown was of rich white silk, covered with exquisite Alençon. As she had legally been Empress since the previous evening, the Crown Jewels of France had been placed at her disposal, and she thus wore a *boucle de ceinture* simulating a sun, the historic Regent or Pitt diamond forming the planet, and three hundred other brilliants figuring its rays or hanging as *aiguillettes.* Further, a diadem of six hundred brilliants bedimmed the effulgence of her hair, whence, from under a spray of orange-blossom, fell a veil of Brussels point. A rope of pearls, her own property, was wound four times round her fair young neck. And to all the splendour of jewels and raiment was added the grace of a born queen. . . .

The Emperor and Empress—he in full uniform and wearing the collar of the Legion of Honour and the Golden Fleece—went together in a great coach, surmounted by an imperial crown and elaborately gilded and adorned with paintings, which had been built for the wedding of Napoleon I and Marie Louise. But at the outset a curious and ominous mishap occurred. The bridal pair had taken their seats, and the vehicle was passing under the vaulted entrance of the Tuileries into the courtyard, when the imperial crown suddenly fell from the coach to the ground. The eight horses were at once halted, the crown was picked up, and in some fashion or other set in place again. . . . A virtually identical accident had occurred with the same coach and the same carriage at the marriage of Napoleon I and Marie Louise.

It was not the only inauspicious augury that day. A Spanish lady who witnessed the wedding expressed her amazement that the Empress, being a Spaniard, should have ventured to wear a rope of pearls, for, according to an old Castillian saying, "The pearls that women wear on their wedding-day symbolize the tears they are fated to shed."

From "*The Court of the Tuileries*"
by Le Petit Homme Rouge.

II

Queen Victoria on Sundry Occasions

She came into the Abbey on her Coronation Day "as gay as a lark, like a girl on her birthday," wearing a diamond circlet and the Parliament robes of crimson velvet, ermine and gold lace, fastened with a gold cord with tassels; eight train-bearers in white and silver followed her. When she had taken the oath to maintain the Protestant reformed religion, she went to St Edward's Chapel, where she changed into a linen gown and a garment called the supertunica. This was of cloth of gold and silver, lined with crimson silk, and richly embroidered with roses and shamrocks and thistles and palms. It suited the young Queen admirably.

On her wedding day she wore white satin trimmed with Honiton. Her wreath of orange-blossom and a sapphire brooch had been given her by Prince Albert. When the bride and groom left to drive to Windsor Castle where they were spending the honeymoon, she was wearing white silk trimmed with swansdown, and a bonnet so deep that it hid her little face. Eighteen years later Victoria wore lilac and silver at the wedding of her eldest daughter, the Princess Royal. This child-bride, who was to become the Empress of Germany, was married in white *moiré*, trimmed like her mother's wedding-dress with Honiton lace. The trousseau the young bride was taking to Germany included twenty pairs of galoshes.

III

The Coronation Dress of H.M. Queen Elizabeth the Second

Mr Norman Hartnell who designed the dress describes the material as pure white satin; but Miss Audrey Russell, who described it on more than one occasion over the radio, tells us that the general impression of the colour was very pale gold. This was due to the background embroidery of lattice-work, in seed pearls, crystals and gold thread, with which the dress was entirely encrusted. Here and there were touches of soft greens, pale pinks and pale yellows, where the embroidered emblems of Britain and the Commonwealth were superimposed on the lattice-work design.

The bodice, sleeves and extreme hem were bordered with a wide embroidered band of golden crystals, graduated diamonds and pearls. This motif was repeated three times in festoons across the full flared skirt to enclose the emblems belonging to each country. The Tudor Rose of England predominated, in palest pink, pearls, and gold and silver bullion. The Welsh Leek appeared in white silk and diamonds. The Irish Shamrock in green silk, diamonds and silver thread. The Scottish Thistle was represented in pale mauve silk and amethysts, with the calyx in reseda green silk, silver thread, and diamond dewdrops.

In one panel of the skirt every emblem of the Commonwealth countries closely surrounded the Tudor Rose. In 1953, the year of the Coronation, these included Canada, Australia, New Zealand, South Africa, India, Pakistan, and Ceylon; so the maple leaf, the fern, the wattle, the protea, lotus flowers, cotton and jute flowers were all part of the embroidered design.

Thousands of people in the Commonwealth countries had the opportunity of seeing the Queen wearing this historic and sumptuous dress during her World Tour after the Coronation. Regardless of tropical temperatures the Queen attended special sessions of Parliament in Wellington, Canberra, and Colombo wearing her Coronation gown. It surpassed in splendour, though perhaps not in beauty, the lovely Wedding dress, also designed for her by Norman Hartnell, in which the floral designs were inspired by Botticelli's *Primavera*.

On this occasion, when she was still a Princess, the Queen's Bridal Bouquet was presented to her by the Worshipful Company of Gardeners. Not everyone who saw it knew that it contained a link with the past. For when Mr Martin Longman, the florist, took the bouquet to the Palace on the morning of the Wedding, he was given a small sprig of myrtle, and asked to include it with the Odontoglossum orchids and other white flowers. It came from Queen Victoria's garden at Osborne.

With thanks to Miss Audrey Russell,
a Queen of Commentators

Half a Loaf is Better than No Bread

EDWARD THOMAS

Edward Thomas was a Welsh writer who died in the First World War before he grew old. He was a great walker and a great reader, and loved all that was best to be found in the open air and in books. Best of all he loved poetry, but he did not write any till the last three years of his life. Before that he wrote about poets and nature and legends and other things that have poetry in them. At first, when he began to write poems himself, he kept them a secret from his friends. They were not published till after he died, and he became famous for them; but he never knew that one day the world would think of him as another Thomas the Rhymer, like the poet in this story.

E.F.

THOMAS the Rhymer was in Fairyland seven years. As he was lying one May-day on Huntly Bank he saw a beautiful lady come riding towards him under Eildon Tree. So wonderful was her beauty that he knelt down in the fern before her, thinking she was Mary, the mother of Jesus. But she told him not to kneel to her. She was not Mary Queen of Heaven, but the Queen of Fairyland. She had come there to see him because she had heard that he was a wise man who could foretell the future. Thomas looked at her again, at her face that was as bright as moss on snow, at her dress of grass-green silk and her jewels, and her horn of gold, and the falcon upon her wrist, at the silver bells hanging from the braids of her horse's mane, which was white, and at the hounds in the fern round about. She was so beautiful that he was willing to do anything she might ask. A second time he knelt to her, telling her he loved her and would go with her anywhere. She smiled and let him mount the horse behind her before she told him that if he came with her he would not be home again for seven years. Thomas had not lived so long that he could not spare seven years for the Queen of Fairyland; so together they rode away from Huntly Bank, day and night, through a land where they saw neither sun nor moon, but heard the sea roaring, until they came to a garden. From one of the apple-trees growing there the Queen plucked an apple for Thomas. "This," said she, "is your wages. The man who eats this cannot lie." "Alas," replied Thomas, "that may be well in Fairyland; but what shall I do in the world if I cannot lie?" The Queen scolded him: "Why should you think of the world when you have seven years of Fairyland before you? Would you lie to me? Did you lie when you said you loved me more than all women?" Thomas ate the apple, and put on the green cloth and the green shoes of Fairyland.

So much everyone knows; Thomas told it to all that asked him. But what happened in those seven years, why he came back to Scotland, whether he was glad to be back, no man pretends to know. Yet this one thing also has been told. All his friends had long given Thomas up for lost, except his mother. Every day she baked one of the small loaves that her son loved best, in case he should come home again. Every evening she cut the loaf in two to give half to a beggar; and next morning the other half went to Thomas's old dog.

Now, as chance would have it, Thomas returned at last

on Midsummer night; and this is the thing that is told of him after his home-coming. When his mother saw him she cried out, partly for joy, partly for sorrow that she had only half a loaf left. She hardly found time to kiss her son, so much was she troubled about the bread. Thomas comforted her as best he could, though he was True Thomas now, and could not lie. "Mother," he said, "it's not for a man who has been seven years in Fairyland, and found his way home again, to complain about the bread; and in any case half a loaf is better than no bread." After this he began to eat. Perhaps the bread took away his memory of Fairyland. Who knows? At least we know that True Thomas declared that half a loaf is better than no bread.

Queen Alice

LEWIS CARROLL

Lewis Carroll taught the harder kinds of arithmetic at the University of Oxford; but you wouldn't expect it if you had only read about Alice. There is, though, a little *arithmetic in Alice, of a simple kind, like, "What's one and one and one and one and one and one and one and one and one and one?" I'm sorry to say that Alice didn't know. However, that's in the story, and, since Alice was a queen by then it was her duty to know. She had been travelling all day across a strange country of square fields and woods with little brooks between; and she had met knights and kings and gnats and things, and an Anglo-Saxon messenger. She was* in *a game of chess, you see. She wasn't playing it: it was playing her. Then she came to a brook, and bounded across—and it was the last square, and . . . Well, if you can get a pawn right across the chessboard, on to the eighth square, you can turn it into a Queen, and that is what happened to Alice. She threw herself down on the grass, and lifted from her head the heavy thing that had just got there.*

It was a golden crown.

W.M.

"WELL, this *is* grand!" said Alice. "I never expected I should be a Queen so soon—and I'll tell you what it is, your Majesty," she went on, in a severe tone (she was always rather fond of scolding herself), "it'll never do for you to be lolling about on the grass like that! Queens have to be dignified, you know!"

So she got up and walked about—rather stiffly just at first, as she was afraid that the crown might come off: but she comforted herself with the thought that there was nobody to see her, "and if I really am a Queen," she said as she sat down again, "I shall be able to manage it quite well in time."

Everything was happening so oddly that she didn't feel a bit surprised at finding the Red Queen and the White Queen sitting close to her, one on each side: she would have liked very much to ask them how they came there, but she feared it would not be quite civil. However, there would be no harm, she thought, in asking if the game was over. "Please, would you tell me—" she began, looking timidly at the Red Queen.

"Speak when you're spoken to!" the Queen sharply interrupted her.

"But if everybody obeyed that rule," said Alice, who was always ready for a little argument, "and if you only spoke when you were spoken to, and the other person always waited for *you* to begin, you see nobody would ever say anything, so that—"

"Ridiculous!" cried the Queen. "Why, don't you see, child—" here she broke off with a frown, and, after thinking for a minute, suddenly changed the subject of the conversation. "What do you mean by 'If you really are a Queen'? What right have you to call yourself so? You can't be a Queen, you know, till you've passed the proper examination. And the sooner we begin it, the better."

"I only said 'if'!" poor Alice pleaded in a piteous tone.

The two Queens looked at each other, and the Red Queen remarked, with a little shudder, "She *says* she only said 'if'—"

"But she said a great deal more than that!" the White Queen moaned, wringing her hands. "Oh, ever so much more than that!"

"So you did, you know," the Red Queen said to Alice. "Always speak the truth—think before you speak—and write it down afterwards."

"I'm sure I didn't mean—" Alice was beginning, but the Red Queen interrupted her impatiently.

"That's just what I complain of! You *should* have meant! What do you suppose is the use of a child without any meaning? Even a joke should have some meaning—and a child's more important than a joke, I hope. You couldn't deny that, even if you tried with both hands."

"I don't deny things with my *hands*," Alice objected.

"Nobody said you did," said the Red Queen. "I said you couldn't if you tried."

"She's in that state of mind," said the White Queen, "that she wants to deny *something*—only she doesn't know what to deny!"

"A nasty, vicious temper," the Red Queen remarked; and then there was an uncomfortable silence for a minute or two.

The Red Queen broke the silence by saying, to the White Queen, "I invite you to Alice's dinner-party this afternoon."

The White Queen smiled feebly, and said, "And I invite *you*."

"I didn't know I was to have a party at all," said Alice; "but, if there *is* to be one, I think *I* ought to invite the guests."

"We gave you the opportunity of doing it," the Red Queen remarked: "but I daresay you've not had many lessons in manners yet."

"Manners are not taught in lessons," said Alice. "Lessons teach you to do sums, and things of that sort."

"Can you do Addition?" the White Queen asked.

"What's one and one and one and one and one and one and one and one and one and one?"

"I don't know," said Alice. "I lost count."

"She can't do Addition," the Red Queen interrupted. "Can you do Subtraction? Take nine from eight."

"Nine from eight I can't, you know," Alice replied very readily: "but—"

"She can't do Subtraction," said the White Queen. "Can you do Division? Divide a loaf by a knife—what's the answer to that?"

"I suppose—" Alice was beginning, but the Red Queen answered for her. "Bread-and-butter, of course. Try another Subtraction sum. Take a bone from a dog: what remains?"

Alice considered. "The bone wouldn't remain, of course, if I took it—and the dog wouldn't remain: it would come to bite me—and I'm sure I shouldn't remain!"

"Then you think nothing would remain?" said the Red Queen.

"I think that's the answer."

"Wrong, as usual," said the Red Queen: "the dog's temper would remain."

"But I don't see how—"

"Why, look here!" the Red Queen cried. "The dog would lose its temper, wouldn't it?"

"Perhaps it would," Alice replied cautiously.

"Then if the dog went away, its temper would remain!" the Queen exclaimed triumphantly.

Alice said, as gravely as she could, "They might go different ways." But she couldn't help thinking to herself "What dreadful nonsense we *are* talking!"

"She can't do sums a *bit*!" the Queens said together, with great emphasis.

"Can *you* do sums?" Alice said, turning suddenly on the White Queen, for she didn't like being found fault with so much.

The Queen gasped and shut her eyes. "I can do Addition," she said, "if you give me time—but I can't do Subtraction under *any* circumstances!"

"Of course you know your ABC?" said the Red Queen.

"To be sure I do," said Alice.

"So do I," the White Queen whispered: "we'll often say it over together, dear. And I'll tell you a secret—I can read words of one letter! Isn't *that* grand? However, don't be discouraged. You'll come to it in time."

Here the Red Queen began again. "Can you answer useful questions?" she said. "How is bread made?"

"I know *that*!" Alice cried eagerly. "You take some flour—"

"Where do you pick the flower?" the White Queen asked: "in a garden or in the hedges?"

"Well, it isn't *picked* at all," Alice explained: "it's *ground*—"

"How many acres of ground?" said the White Queen. "You mustn't leave out so many things."

"Fan her head!" the Red Queen anxiously interrupted. "She'll be feverish after so much thinking." So they set to work and fanned her with bunches of leaves, till she had to beg them to leave off, it blew her hair about so.

"She's all right again now," said the Red Queen. "Do you know Languages? What's the French for fiddle-de-dee?"

"Fiddle-de-dee's not English," Alice replied gravely.

"Whoever said it was?" said the Red Queen.

Alice thought she saw a way out of the difficulty, this time. "If you'll tell me what language 'fiddle-de-dee' is,

I'll tell you the French for it!" she exclaimed triumphantly.

But the Red Queen drew herself up rather stiffly, and said, "Queens never make bargains."

"I wish Queens never asked questions," Alice thought to herself.

"Don't let us quarrel," the White Queen said in an anxious tone. "What is the cause of lightning?"

"The cause of lightning," Alice said very decidedly, for she felt quite certain about this, "is the thunder—no, no!" she hastily corrected herself. "I meant the other way."

"It's too late to correct it," said the Red Queen: "when you've once said a thing, that fixes it, and you must take the consequences."

"Which reminds me—" the White Queen said, looking down and nervously clasping and unclasping her hands, "we had *such* a thunderstorm last Tuesday—I mean one of the last set of Tuesdays, you know."

Alice was puzzled. "In *our* country," she remarked, "there's only one day at a time."

The Red Queen said, "That's a poor thin way of doing things. Now *here*, we mostly have days and nights two or three at a time, and sometimes in the winter we take as many as five nights together—for warmth, you know."

"Are five nights warmer than one night, then?" Alice ventured to ask.

"Five times as warm, of course."

"But they should be five times as *cold*, by the same rule—"

"Just so!" cried the Red Queen. "Five times as warm, *and* five times as cold—just as I'm five times as rich as you are, *and* five times as clever!"

Alice sighed and gave it up. "It's exactly like a riddle with no answer!" she thought.

"Humpty Dumpty saw it too," the White Queen went on in a low voice, more as if she were talking to herself. "He came to the door with a corkscrew in his hand—"

"What did he want?" said the Red Queen.

"He said he *would* come in," the White Queen went on, "because he was looking for a hippopotamus. Now, as it happened, there wasn't such a thing in the house, that morning."

"Is there generally?" Alice asked in an astonished tone.

"Well, only on Thursdays," said the Queen.

"I know what he came for," said Alice: "he wanted to punish the fish, because—"

Here the White Queen began again, "It was *such* a thunderstorm, you can't think!" ("She *never* could, you know," said the Red Queen.) "And part of the roof came off, and ever so much thunder got in—and it went rolling round the room in great lumps—and knocking over the tables and things—till I was so frightened, I couldn't remember my own name!"

Alice thought to herself, "I never should *try* to remember my name in the middle of an accident! Where would be the use of it?" but she did not say this aloud, for fear of hurting the poor Queen's feelings.

"Your Majesty must excuse her," the Red Queen said to Alice, taking one of the White Queen's hands in her own, and gently stroking it: "she means well, but she can't help saying foolish things as a general rule."

The White Queen looked timidly at Alice, who felt she *ought* to say something kind, but really couldn't think of anything at the moment.

"She never was really well brought up," the Red Queen went on: "but it's amazing how good-tempered she is! Pat her on the head, and see how pleased she'll be!"

But this was more than Alice had courage to do.

"A little kindness—and putting her hair in papers—would do wonders with her—"

The White Queen gave a deep sigh, and laid her head on Alice's shoulder. "I *am* so sleepy!" she moaned.

"She's tired, poor thing!" said the Red Queen. "Smooth her hair—lend her your nightcap—and sing her a soothing lullaby."

"I haven't got a nightcap with me," said Alice, as she tried to obey the first direction: "and I don't know any soothing lullabies."

"I must do it myself, then," said the Red Queen, and she began:

"Hush-a-by lady, in Alice's lap!
Till the feast's ready, we've time for a nap.
When the feast's over, we'll go to the ball—
Red Queen, and White Queen, and Alice, and all!

"And now you know the words," she added, as she put her head down on Alice's other shoulder, "just sing it through to *me*. I'm getting sleepy, too." In another moment both Queens were fast asleep, and snoring loud.

"What *am* I to do?" exclaimed Alice, looking about in great perplexity, as first one round head, and then the other, rolled down from her shoulder, and lay like a heavy lump in her lap. "I don't think it *ever* happened before, that anyone had to take care of two Queens asleep at once! No, not in all the History of England—it couldn't, you know, because there never was more than one Queen at a time. Do wake up, you heavy things!" she went on in an impatient tone; but there was no answer but a gentle snoring.

The snoring got more distinct every minute, and

sounded more like a tune: at last she could even make out words, and she listened so eagerly that, when the two great heads suddenly vanished from her lap, she hardly missed them. She was standing before an arched doorway, over which were the words "Queen Alice" in large letters, and on each side of the arch there was a bell-handle; one was marked "Visitors' Bell", and the other "Servants' Bell".

"I'll wait till the song's over," thought Alice, "and then I'll ring the—the— *which* bell must I ring?" she went on, very much puzzled by the names. "I'm not a visitor, and I'm not a servant. There *ought* to be one marked 'Queen', you know—"

Just then the door opened a little way, and a creature with a long beak put its head out for a moment and said, "No admittance till the week after next!" and shut the door again with a bang.

Alice knocked and rang in vain for a long time; but at last a very old Frog, who was sitting under a tree, got up and hobbled slowly towards her: he was dressed in bright yellow, and had enormous boots on.

"What is it, now?" the Frog said in a deep hoarse whisper.

Alice turned round, ready to find fault with anybody. "Where's the servant whose business it is to answer the door?" she began angrily.

"Which door?" said the Frog.

Alice almost stamped with irritation at the slow drawl in which he spoke. "*This* door, of course!"

The Frog looked at the door with his large dull eyes for a minute: then he went nearer and rubbed it with his thumb, as if he were trying whether the paint would come off: then he looked at Alice.

"To answer the door?" he said. "What's it been asking

of?" He was so hoarse that Alice could scarcely hear him.

"I don't know what you mean," she said.

"I speaks English, doesn't I?" the Frog went on. "Or are you deaf? What did it ask you?"

"Nothing!" Alice said impatiently. "I've been knocking at it!"

"Shouldn't do that—shouldn't do that—" the Frog muttered. "Wexes it, you know." Then he went up and gave the door a kick with one of his great feet. "You let *it* alone," he panted out, as he hobbled back to his tree, "and it'll let *you* alone, you know."

At this moment the door was flung open, and a shrill voice was heard singing:

"To the Looking-Glass world it was Alice that said
'I've a sceptre in hand, I've a crown on my head.
Let the Looking-Glass creatures, whatever they be
Come and dine with the Red Queen, the White Queen, and me!' "

And hundreds of voices joined in the chorus:

"Then fill up the glasses as quick as you can,
And sprinkle the table with buttons and bran:
Put cats in the coffee and mice in the tea—
And welcome Queen Alice with thirty-times-three!"

Then followed a confused noise of cheering, and Alice thought to herself "Thirty times three makes ninety. I wonder if anyone's counting?" In a minute there was silence again, and the same shrill voice sang another verse:

" 'O Looking-Glass creatures', quoth Alice, 'draw near!
'Tis an honour to see me, a favour to hear:
'Tis a privilege high to have dinner and tea
Along with the Red Queen, the White Queen, and me!' "

Then came the chorus again:

"Then fill up the glasses with treacle and ink,
Or anything else that is pleasant to drink:
Mix sand with the cider, and wool with the wine—
And welcome Queen Alice with ninety-times-nine!"

"Ninety times nine!" Alice repeated in despair. "Oh, that'll never be done! I'd better go in at once—" and in she went, and there was a dead silence the moment she appeared.

The Queen's Free Day

Jane Bowers.

One day quite unexpectedly the queen had a free day so she thought that she would go by bus to the cinema. When she got to the Bus Stop there was a long queue and she had to wait a little while. Presently she managed to get on a bus and go

on her way. When
she got to the cinema
she saw that it
was a film on the
Ballet, the queen was
very pleased. After the
film was over the
queen went to a
Wimpy House. She
chose to have Wimpy
and Chips. There were
many people in the
Wimpy House. Then
the Queen went to
see a new church,
she said a fervent

prayer and then she went to see some friends. Fiist she went to see 41, Derwent Avenue to visit Mrs Applepie, who was a great friend of hers. Mrs Applepie was having Central Heating installed and she had new cupboards and a dressing table. The Queen admired, all this and gave helpful advice. Having made one friend feel happy she went to 72, Vanna Street to visit Mrs Buddle. Mrs Buddle was having some new furniture arriving so the queen admired this. Then the Queen went to 84, Pineapple Road, where Mrs & Mr Peartree were having a new Sink Unit put in this too was admired. Next the Queen went to see Mrs Mudpie. Mrs Mudpie was dusting the window when the Queen walked up her path and when she saw who it was she was speechless with delight. The Queen's last visit was to Mrs Pinetree who lived in the middle of London. Her flat was No 70 and it was right at the top of the block of flats.

The Queen did not
take the Lift but
climbed all the
stairs and knocked
on the door. Mrs
Pinetree was having
High Tea, she got up
from her chair and
opened the door and
to her joy and
astonishment saw the
Queen. She asked
her in and they
had a drink of
wine and the queen
shared Mrs Pinetree's

High Tea as by
now she had
forgotten all about
her Wimpy and Chips
and was rather
hungry. The two
friends had a lovely
chat. The queen then
went home to her
husband feeling so
happy and satisfied
at having visited
some good old
friends. That evening
she told her husband
all about her free

day and he said
"You must do it
more often my dear!"

The Queen of Sheba

From the first Book of Kings—Chapter 10.

AND when the queen of Sheba heard of the fame of Solomon concerning the name of the LORD, she came to prove him with hard questions.

And she came to Jerusalem with a very great train, with camels that bare spices, and very much gold, and precious stones: and when she was come to Solomon, she communed with him of all that was in her heart.

And Solomon told all her questions: there was not any thing hid from the king, which he told her not.

And when the queen of Sheba had seen all Solomon's wisdom, and the house that he had built,

And the meat of his table, and the sitting of his servants, and the attendance of his ministers, and their apparel, and his cupbearers, and his ascent by which he went up unto the house of the LORD: there was no more spirit in her.

And she said to the king, It was a true report that I heard in mine own land of thy acts and of thy wisdom.

Howbeit I believed not the words, until I came, and mine eyes had seen it: and, beheld, the half was not told me: thy wisdom and prosperity exceedeth the fame which I heard.

Happy are thy men, happy are these thy servants, which stand continually before thee, and that hear thy wisdom.

Blessed be the LORD thy God, which delighted in thee, to set thee on the throne of Israel: because the LORD loved Israel for ever, therefore made he thee king, to do judgment and justice.

And she gave the king an hundred and twenty talents of gold, and of spices very great store, and precious stones: there came no more such abundance of spices as these which the queen of Sheba gave to king Solomon.

And the navy also of Hiram, that brought gold from Ophir, brought in from Ophir great plenty of almug trees, and precious stones.

And the king made of almug trees pillars for the house of the LORD, and for the king's house, harps also for psalteries for singers: there came no such almug trees, nor were seen unto this day.

And king Solomon gave unto the queen of Sheba all her desire, whatsoever she asked beside that which Solomon gave her of his royal bounty. So she turned and went to her own country, she and her servants.

Gone

WALTER DE LA MARE

Where's the Queen of Sheba
Where King Solomon?
Gone with Boy Blue who looks after the sheep,
Gone and gone and gone.

Lovely is the sunshine;
Lovely is the wheat;
Lovely the wind from out of the clouds
Having its way with it.

Rise up, Old Green-Stalks!
Delve deep, Old Corn!
But where's the Queen of Sheba?
Where King Solomon?

BOUND
HUNTTING